I0533036

Unconditional

A collection of feel good stories

Silvano Stagni

Perpetual Mobile Limited

Copyright © 2023 by Silvano Stagni

All rights reserved. No part of this publication may be reproduced, stored or transmitted in any form or by any means, electronic, mechanical, photocopying, recording, scanning, or otherwise without written permission from the publisher. It is illegal to copy this book, post it to a website, or distribute it by any other means without permission, except for the use of brief quotations in a book review.

This collection of short story is entirely a work of fiction. The names, characters and incidents portrayed in it are the work of the author's imagination. Any resemblance to actual persons, living or dead, events or localities is entirely coincidental.

 Created with Vellum

To the memory of my mother, who taught me to take people as they are and not as what anyone else wants them to be.

The Pond

A tale of recollections and acceptance

Gabriel loved the view from the study; he always did. His first memory of that view was when he was five; they had just arrived at his grandfather's for one of the long summer weekends. He had moved to the family holiday home after his wife had passed away. Gabriel's father had barely turned off the engine of the car, and they saw his grandfather emerging from a swim in the pond. He was seventy-two then and looked like a white-haired Neptune. He welcomed them and excused himself to go and get dressed. When he reappeared, there were refreshments laid out in his study. At the time, Gabriel could not understand why his grandfather did not use the swimming pool. He dreamed of a private swimming pool, something easier to achieve when you have a lot of land around the house than if you live in a city.

* * *

One could only see half of the pond from the study; a large terrace was obstructing the view of the other half. In reality, "the pond" was a large artificial lake created by a landscape architect commissioned by Gabriel's great-great-grandfather after he saw an English stately home during a visit to London in the 1880s. It had three follies and two picnic areas around its perimeter. Gabriel had proposed to his wife in one of the fake ruins around the lake.

Gabriel and Ruth were staying at his grandfather's for a long weekend in October. Gabriel wanted to show his girlfriend the colour of nature transitioning from Summer to Winter. Ruth had been there before; Gabriel's grandfather liked her. They had been walking around the pond and had reached the picnic table by the fake Roman ruins. Gabriel had prepared the basked when Ruth was in the shower getting ready for the last day before going back to university. He had included a portable record player in the basket. Ruth was looking at the shades of green and yellow in the water, the reflection of the surrounding trees in the pond. She was surprised to hear music, she turned around, and Gabriel was on one knee, holding a ring. The dialogue was repeated several times during their married life. She mercilessly teased him.

"Are you asking?"

"Yes, what are you answering?"

"Yes"

When they walked back, they realised that Gabriel's grandfather had been watching the scene from the terrace. His reaction was priceless. He had a bottle of champagne on ice and three glasses.

"I already rang your parents. They are drinking champagne as we speak, and so shall we."

Unfortunately, he passed away in his mid-nineties, a year before they got married.

* * *

The day showed the first hint of spring, the snow in the garden was beginning to melt, but the pond was still frozen. Gabriel made a mental note to ask the gardener to check if the ice was still thick enough to skate. His grandchildren were due that evening, and he knew they would want to skate.

After his parents passed away, Gabriel made very few changes to the study. It was a room cherished by many generations of his family, and he felt very safe there. Indirect memories framed and hung were competing for space with the books and direct memories firmly framed in his mind. Turning the big leather armchairs towards the window was the only change he made. He could not care less who else was in the room; he loved the view of the pond.

His late wife, a native New Yorker, did as well; it reminded her of the lake in Central Park. She liked it frozen, though. Snow-covered trees and a frozen pond were her ideas of home. Long before they moved to the house, she had a framed photograph of the frozen pond in their bedroom. She always did. Roy took it a couple of years after his mother died. Gabriel preferred the summer. He loved swimming in the pond like his grandfather used to do. He did not fancy himself a dark blond Neptune, but he thought of his grandfather every time he emerged from the pond looking for the towel.

Gabriel went back to his book. After a few more pages, the music he had in the background took him back to memory lane. He remembered when they arrived to visit his parents.

His father had received a phone call from a friend who had seen them when they stopped to fill the car. His mother had been lingering by the door, waiting to welcome them. Gabriel's daughters barely waited for the car to stop and jumped out to greet their grandmother. Jonathan, his younger son, was in his "too cool for school" mode and took his time. His daughters still had not found their volume control, so when their grandfather appeared, summoned by the noise, they enthusiastically went from loud to louder to greet him. Myriam and Susan were trying to extract a promise from him to take out the boat the following day. They had not taken out the luggage from the trunk of the car yet when they heard the noise of another vehicle. Roy had arrived with Simon. Gabriele and Ruth exchanged worried looks; it was the first time Roy would have taken his partner to meet his grandparents. They both wondered how they would react to their eldest grandson being gay. Gabriel's parents did not hesitate for a second; they smiled when Roy introduced Simon. Then Roy's grandfather stood in the middle of the two young men, put an arm on their shoulder, pulled both to him, and welcomed Simon in the traditional family way, with a hug. His wife was less theatrical; she hugged and kissed both on their forehead, welcomed Roy, took Simon's arm, and led him inside, asking him what his favourite dishes were.

Gabriel was sure that his parents would not have had a problem with Roy's introducing his partner. His mother had always maintained that "your sexual tastes are none of my business as long as you deal with consenting adults." His father was slightly more direct "if I am not involved, they can do what they want." By the end of the weekend, they had fallen in love with Simon, and Simon had fallen in love with them. From that moment on, the relationship grew stronger and stronger.

* * *

Beethoven's triple concert had finished; the end of the music brought Gabriel back to the here and now. He stood up and looked for the next CD to put on; somehow, the memory of Simon's introduction drew him to pick the Magic Flute. After all, Roy once described Simon as "his male Papagena".

Roy had invited himself and Simon for dinner on Friday night; they had something they wanted to tell them. Myriam, the least patient in the family, kept asking what their news was; each time, Roy patiently told her to wait until the end of the meal. Finally, he announced that they had decided to have a commitment ceremony waiting for the day they could get married. Susan and Myriam hugged Roy; Ruth turned to Simon with a serious face.

"Did he ask you? Because his father just showed me the ring."

All the children had heard the story many times. They smiled and everybody rolled their eyes when Ruth proceeded to tell it to Simon, who, maybe out of politeness or maybe out of curiosity, had asked what happened. Somehow champagne appeared, and the atmosphere could not have been happier. The following Sunday, Simon's parents' reaction to the idea was definitely frosty. They decided to leave after lunch. Simon asked Roy to take him to see his grandparents. As they were filling up at a service station, Roy called his grandparents to announce their impending arrival; Simon was not within earshot, so he summarised the frosty lunch. Their reception could not have been warmer. At the end of the evening, Simon asked if he could stay a couple of days. He would take the train back. He needed to feel accepted and loved. As usual, Roy's grandfather hugged him; Roy's grandmother was more pragmatic. She thought that Roy's spare clothes would fit him, and she would organise to clean the clothes Simon was wearing so he could wear them on the journey back to town.

* * *

The end of The Magic Flute interrupted the trip down memory lane for a few minutes. He selected a playlist from the internet, filled his glass, and sat back, but the book stayed closed on the table. He turned to the empty leather armchair on the other side of the small table, he still missed his late wife. The memory of his wife brought other memories and he sort of remember the conversation he had with his wife about what to do with the family estate.

They were having lunch on the terrace; they did not know yet but Ruth was already sick. She was feeling fine and blamed any malaise to her age.

"I would like to leave the holiday house to Roy and Simon, with the provision that his siblings can use it whenever they like. What do you think?"

Ruth put down the cutlery, took a sip of water and looked at him in silence. Gabriel knew she was thinking, looking at him in silence was her way to buy time.

"I agree, they seem to be the ones that have the strongest bond with this place. They also the ones who are better off. If you leave the house to them, you can divide everything else among the other three. Roy and Simon love this place, so they should not feel they missed out on the rest. Following the same logic, you might want to leave our city home to Susan. Jonathan and Myriam need to receive enough to compensate them for not having a share in this house or in the flat."

I have something in mind, but I will write to each of them detailing my ideas and then check that they think it is a fair subdivision of the estate.

Gabriel was happy he had a good relationship with all his children. Some relationships were warmer than others, but everybody still showed up for his birthday weekend, and they called frequently. He could not complain. Roy and Susan were the closest to him, the ones who still lived in the country. When he and Ruth decided it was time to leave the city, Roy and Simon had helped them move. Roy had to go back to work, and the children had to return to school, but Simon had stayed for a couple of days longer without the children to make sure they had settled. Roy and Simon loved the house, it definitely was in good hands with them. Gabriel was looking forward to their visit tonight. Somehow his children and other friends made sure he was never alone during the weekend. They would usually arrive with the Friday night meal. He took another sip of his drink and noticed a swan by the pond. Maybe it was not safe for Lisa to skate the following day. He had to tell Roy and Simon they had to check with the gardener before they even started negotiating with Lisa. He knew she was as good at getting what she wanted out of everybody at seventeen as when she was five. Thinking of his granddaughter reminded him of the summer when Simon and Roy were visiting on the same weekend when Susan and her husband were there.

They had gone for a walk around the Pond and stopped at one of the picnic tables to talk. Gabriel was reading, sitting on a deckchair on the terrace, when Ruth came out to tell him that it was too hot to prepare dinner; his mother had organised a cold meal. She pointed at their children and sons-in-law.

"Just let me know when they start heading back and then come and help me take everything out here; I guess they'll tell us what they talked about over dinner if it is important."

It turned out it was important. Susan had volunteered to donate eggs so Roy and Simon could have children; they would use Simon's sperm so the children will also have 50% of Roy's genetic heritage. A year later, Simon insisted that the twins they had through a surrogate be named Lisa and Michael to honour Roy's grandparents. Gabriel smiled, thinking how happy and proud his parents would be to hear the news. They agreed to keep quiet and let Simon tell them when they came to see the babies. Their reaction was priceless. Gabriel's father decided that from that moment on, he was "Big Michael" then, he looked at his wife with a naughty grin and added, "You will be old Lisa". A comment that did not exactly go down well with Gabriel's mother

Susan's mother-in-law, Hanna, had been equally enthusiastic.

"Susan and Joshua have told me they are almost ready to start having children. Until that happens I will practice being a grandmother with these two."

Simon's comment temporarily moved her to tears.

"Well, they are not going to see my parents much, do you mind being their grandmother even when Susan and Joshua have children?"

Hanna looked at him, fighting tears. She simply hugged him and said

"Only if you allow me to be a mother figure for you"

* * *

Gabriel realised the music had ended. He went to the CD player and put the CD back in the box. Lisa and Michael and their fathers would spend the weekend with him; he'd better make sure that everything he was keen on was in its proper place before the hurricane grandchildren descended on the property. Thinking of chaos, he remembered the day Roy and Simon got married.

It was the first same-sex wedding celebrated in the small town where the house was located, a month after the law had passed. The council had suggested a wedding in the garden of the house; it would have been more private and less controversial. Simon and Roy had walked down the aisle together, their children between them. Jonathan had one ring, and Susan had the other. A very pregnant Myriam followed, surrounded by all the grandchildren. Simon's parents were not there. Susan's mother-in-law was "the other mother of the groom" after all, Ruth could not divide herself into two, and Hanna was Simon and Roy's children other grandmother. Moreover, it was not fair that Ruth had all the fun.

* * *

He went back to his book. After a while, his head felt heavy; he put down the drink and closed his eyes. The book was resting on his lap. His dream was bizarre; his four children were having a picnic on the terrace off the small fake theatre built in a style that mimicked a Palladian villa. They were all there with their spouses and children; he saw it as a film. He felt very happy; he had four children and eleven grandchildren. Then, they were still having a picnic, but he was swimming in the pond. He stopped to wave at them, and they all waved back smiling, the grandchildren encouraging him. He continued swimming; he realised he was swimming towards Ruth, who was waiting for him by the fake ruins where he had proposed to her all those years ago. She was smiling at him; when he reached her, she simply said: "Don't swim towards the light; it is not time yet." He felt somebody slap his face; he opened his eyes and saw a scared Michael screaming "Grandpa" in-between calling his dads

Lisa, Roy, and Simon rushed in. Simon took his pulse; it was very weak. His son-in-law, the surgeon, took over and decided to take him to the hospital. Gabriel stood up, helped by his grandchildren.

"It is not necessary. Ruth told me it is not time yet."

A new boy in town

I still do not believe it. I work in Wall Street. Well, almost In Wall Street, my office is downtown, on Broadway, half a block away from Wall Street. I have been working there for a month and I still have "pinch me" moments. I had my final interview only three months ago. Now I work near Wall Street and I live in the Upper West Side, half a block from Central Park.

When I walk around in my new neighbourhood I often think of all the movies that were filmed there. Somehow, they wanted me so much that they offered to pay half the rent for five years. I hope that the amount of money I take home will be enough to cover the other half by then. That is assuming I still have a job, and I will still be in New York. One goes with the other.

Today I have to leave the office early, my things have arrived, and I need to be home to take delivery of my bed and my sofa-bed. When I left the office, I flagged a taxi, or – as they say here – I hailed a cab. Telling a cab driver to go to West 72nd between Central Park West and Columbus still sounds odd. Anyway, sitting in the back of a yellow cab, it is one of my "movie-moment." I am definitely still the new boy in town, or at least I am new in this town, I am not sure whether it shows but I am.

I did not bring much from home, just a few pieces with sentimental value, my books, CDs, and a few framed pictures. The bedroom set and sofa-bed will be the first real piece of furniture in my new home. A dining table, chairs, maybe an armchair are the only things missing; wardrobe (or should I say closet?), kitchen with breakfast bar, and bookshelves are all fitted. The company's relocation agent is helping me; other than my colleague, she is the only person I know in New York. I have American friends, but they live elsewhere. So far, there have been promises to introduce me to people they know in New York, but I have been busy during the week and a tourist during the weekend. As a matter of fact, I spent most of my weekends in Central Park with a book, reading and crowd-watching, a lonely figure who hopes to be part of a group one day.

I have never been gregarious by nature; I look forward to being in a room full of people that I do not know almost as I look forward to having a root canal removed. Every time I speak to my mother, she keeps asking me about my social life. A single European Jewish man in New York, if I do not find a Jewish wife here, I don't know where I could find one outside Israel. Adjusting to a new work environment has been my excuse with my mother; I know she hopes to see me move back to Europe with a wife and at least one grandchild.

Meg, the mega-efficient relocation expert who is supposed to hold my hands navigating a new city, will meet me at my flat. It is her last week working with me; after that, I will only be able to count on colleagues and future friends for help. Anyway, utilities, and phone lines, are all connected; I obviously signed the lease of the flat. There is very little left that needs her handholding. Tonight, she will supervise the arrival of the furniture and explain to me how much I am expected to tip. The latter being her excuse to come, the former being the real reason she came.

I ask the cab driver to drop me by Fairway Market on 74th and Broadway. I need to buy some groceries. Somehow walking home with a paper bag full of groceries makes me feel I am inside a romantic comedy. Meg is waiting for me in the lobby; I am still in the romantic comedy for a second. Then she becomes all business; in the lift – I must learn to call it the elevator – she takes out her clipboard with things to do. She goes through the list with me. We must close the fold-up bed and leave it somewhere where it can be easily retrieved. She has already checked that Macy's delivered the bedlinen; we should find the box in the entry hall where the porter put it. Check that the second set of towels has arrived; I may have a washer and dryer in the flat – oooppss apartment – but a second set is helpful. Halfway through the conversation, Meg morphs into my mother; she is a woman a few years older than I am. I shake my head for no apparent reason, and when she asks why I come up with an excuse. I am not telling her that I thought I was hearing my mother's voice. I do not want to give the impression that I am a single Jewish man in his late twenties missing mummy.

Everything arrives; I now am the proud owner of a king-sized bed, bedside tables, chest of drawers, sofa bed, and other things. I pick up a set of stackable tables that somehow found their way into the small container with the other stuff I brought to New York, and I put them next to the sofa bed; a family art deco lamp finds its way on top of the largest of the three. Meg checks that every item on her clipboard is ticked; she will call me in two days for the last item in her hand-holding activities, finding a doctor. I have no idea what they call a General Practitioner over here, but I am sure I'll find out before the end of the week.

Once Meg left, I called a kosher Chinese takeaway and ordered dinner. I still need to equip my kitchen; I am surviving on plastic cups, plastic cutlery, and takeaway dishes. That is a job for next weekend. I sit down waiting for dinner and call my childhood friend Isaac. We were inseparable when we were children in Singapore; we were part of a close-knit group of five boys. Isaac used to live in New York; he got a job with a bank in San Francisco three months before I arrived here. Anyway, he is still at work; he will call me back in the evening, his time.

Half an hour later, when I am dipping chopsticks in a container full of almond chicken next to the one of egg fried rice, my mobile phone rings; I should start calling it cell phone. Ruth – Issacs's mother - is on the phone. She is one of my maternal figures and often reminds me she met me when I was six months old. Since I moved to the US, she has embraced the role of my "American mother." She keeps reminding me that I should think of her home in suburban Washington as my home in the United States and spend a weekend with my "American parents" as soon as I can. I have known her all my life, she treats me like one of her children and it is not weird. I fit in Isaac's family as he fits in mine. Any outsider would think we are part of the same family. I tell her about the furniture and how I fixed it, and she asks me to put the call on video and give her a tour of the place. She makes me promise that I will do the same with my mother; I must call her once we finish our conversation or first thing tomorrow morning before I go to work. She will call her tomorrow to check. I know her well enough to know that it is both a threat and a promise. She will call my mother, and if she finds out I did not call her, I shall have her on the phone, a conversation I am not looking forward to having. She has one final item to discuss with me:

"Do you remember Abby, Isaac's friend from college? I mean his friend, not his girlfriend. Well, she lives in New York. If I remember correctly, she is not far from you. I texted her your phone number, asking her to give you a ring. You are new in town, Isaac is in San Francisco, and you do not know anybody. You may arrange to go to the same synagogue on Shabbat. I must go now. Love you, big hugs, and be good or be very careful... and call your mother! She knows how to use Skype."

The global conspiracy of Jewish mothers is on the case; I will not have a problem having a social life in the Big Apple!

Dad was here

Robert lived about 10 minutes' walk away from his ex-wife's home. Close enough to be able to go back and forth with two small girls, but on different side streets that meant using two different Tube stations to go to work. Robert had a strong intellectual connection with Susan, eight years old, but had a stronger emotional bond with his younger one, Myriam who was five.

It was the end of a weekend with his daughters, a particularly difficult time for Robert. Once they left, he just sat in the living room, switched on the television, did not really pay any notice to what was on. After a while, he got up, went to his daughters' bedroom, turned the light on, looked at the bomb site and went to work. Once order was re-established, Robert put his daughters' bedlinen in the laundry pile, switched the light off, took a shower and went to bed. Sleep was hard to come, he still was not used to being alone in a big bed after ten years of marriage. In the middle of the night he woke up feeling there was somebody else in his bed, he could almost feel this person's head against his shoulder. He was reluctant to turn the light on and surprise the intruder. When he did, there was nobody in his bed, he looked at the bedside clock and noticed it was 4am. He smiled, thought it was a dream and went back to sleep.

Later in the morning, the doorbell surprised him when he was just about coming out of the shower. He put his bathrobe on, went to the window in the study to see who was ringing his doorbell at seven in the morning. He was surprised to see his daughters and their mother. He buzzed them in, turned on the espresso machine (he knew his ex-wife loved coffee) and checked that he still had something for his daughters' breakfast. Susan walked into the kitchen, opened the fridge, took out what she wanted, put it on the kitchen counter, and hugged her father. Myriam directed her mother to lay out the table for breakfast.

They were there because Myriam had woken up around four o'clock screaming, waking up her mother and her sister, When they asked her what happened she kept repeating

"Dad was here, he was. Now he is gone. Dad was asleep in that armchair, I fell asleep hugging him like I used to do when he lived with us. Now he is gone."

Her mother and her sister tried to convince her that it was just a dream. She did not go back to sleep. Her sister had the idea of going to their father's for breakfast so they could show Myriam that her father had slept in his bed; he was not in her room.

Robert reassured Myriam, who left with her mother. He walked Susan to school and then left for work. Standing in the crowded underground train he kept thinking of when he woke up at 4am feeling another person's head against his back. Could people synchronise their dreams?

The love that dare not speak
its name

Richard always felt at home in New York. He had lived there for a few years before moving back to London; his job took him to New York on a regular basis, and he had a social life there. Friends and relatives of his wife had become friends over time. A business trip to New York did not feature the typical solitary evenings in town, and he used the time to see people.

This time it was different; two months earlier, his wife Caroline had told him she wanted a divorce; it came as a complete surprise to him, and his daughters dominated his thoughts. They were still young, and he dreaded being separated from them. He and his wife had agreed they would sell their home and then move to two different homes; the time the house was on the market had been strange. They kept sleeping in the same bed but stopped eating together on weekdays. Weekends traditionally were times to be parents to their two daughters, who were 3 and 6, still too young.

Divorce and finding a place to live large enough to have his daughters stay dominated his thoughts. He was grateful for a demanding job; time at work had become a break from his personal life.

He picked up some of his old routines whenever he was in New York. He usually stayed at a hotel in the Upper West Side, not far from where he used to live and not far from Central Park. The announcement of the separation meant that his ex-wife's friends had politely declined any suggestion to meet; so, a sunny Sunday morning meant a walk in Central park. He took a book like he used to, but his mind was too concerned about the future to read a book. So he decided to sit on one of the benches not far from the 72nd street entrance to the Park, near the Strawberry Fields memorial to John Lennon.

He and Caroline had taken half an hour to sort out the finances; they had done it themselves without a problem. They had few items of contention, most of them books and CDs still available on the market, so each one contributed half the cost of buying them. Time with the children was different; they could not reach an agreement, so Richard sought the advice of a lawyer.

During that warm sunny Sunday in March, Richard could not stop thinking back to his last conversation with his lawyer.

"You'll never get shared residence; you work full time."

He could only reply

"Would you say that to a woman? It is tough to build a case of abuse and violence against me; I always respected my wife."

The lawyer was adamant.

"No, I would not say that to a woman. However, unless you have a case against your wife's behaviour, this is the reality of the family court."

"But I love my daughters; I want to be part of their lives, not just every other weekend!"

Richard thought that it did not matter how sympathetic his solicitor might have sounded; his words still hurt.

"Unfortunately, the family court is not interested in parental love, only in the children's welfare."

That conversation shattered Richard; he felt like giving up going to court and agreeing to whatever Caroline suggested. Sitting at the entrance of the Park, he only noticed men with children or men with pushchairs. He felt that fathers were out in force, like any other sunny Sunday morning in New York. He thought of his daughters, took out his mobile and called Caroline, she did not pick up, yet it was 3 pm in London. He started crying; he could not stop himself.

After a while, he noticed a NYPD woman sitting by his side.

"Is everything all right?"

Richard looked at her, and for a moment, he stopped crying.

"My wife in London wants a divorce. We have two young daughters; I hate the idea of seeing them just on weekends. This morning, I only notice men with children, and I am jealous that they can take their children to the park, and I will only be able to do it every other Sunday."

The NYPD agent was younger than Richard, but she almost looked at him in a maternal way.

"And how do you know that all these men live with their children full-time? For all you know, they could be divorced fathers, and this is the weekend they spend with their children."

Richard smiled behind his tears.

"You are right. I don't know."

The woman looked at him again.

"I divorced three years ago; with my job, my husband could provide a more stable environment for the children. They spend Thursday nights with me and every other weekend. It got better; I felt miserable when they left on a Sunday evening. Now I take them to school on Friday mornings and every other Monday, and I pick them up on Thursdays and every other Friday. I can't say I am used to it, but it got better."

Richard stopped crying

"What hurts is how people react when I say I love my children; it is almost the love that dare not speak his name."

The woman simply said

"It may not be a legal argument, but I am sure your daughters will recognise and appreciate love."

Richard felt a bit better.

"Based on what you say, there is a chance I might adjust. There is nothing I can do now, so I might just sit in the sun and enjoy the book."

"That's the spirit. You are lucky to be in town on such a sunny day in early March; it almost feels like May. Take care, and when you are back in London, hug your daughters on my behalf."

The NYPD woman stood up and continued her beat; she smiled to herself. She understood how Richard felt; three years after her divorce, she still felt the need to say that she loved her children and convince everybody that she did not give them up. Their father could provide a better environment.

Monsoon rain

It is a sweltering summer day in London in the summer of 2020. Living by the river in a flat with big windows facing southwest on a hot and humid day, I feel I am inside a microwave where water is boiling.

A thunder-like noise takes me back more than sixty years to my childhood on the coast of the Indian Ocean in Kenya.

It is the end of the dry season before the long rain; it is very hot. Suddenly, we hear thunder before we see the cloud. Everybody stops what they are doing and waits for the next rumble. You have the feeling that even animals and nature stop.

There is a second thunder, my mother runs outside. We all stand still waiting; a third thunder might give us hope we will finally have some rain.

We are all watching the sky. Humans, animals, and even plants search the sky for clouds. The gardener - everybody's honorary grandpa - points toward the sea: clouds. A breeze starts, gentle and warm; a few seconds later, it is as if somebody had turned on a shower at full blasts.

Plants, animals, and people are all getting wet; my mother and I leave the porch to go outside and start dancing our personal rain dance. We are both soaked, but it does not matter. The hot, dry season is over, it will become unbearably hot and humid in a few days, but now we welcome the rain. We tilt our heads back to get warm rain in our faces; we laugh, we get soaked and do not care. We raise our arms towards the sky and the rain. We are imitating the plants around us that seem to be trying to soak every little drop they can.

Then the rain stops abruptly. We go back inside to dry ourselves; my mother is still laughing. It was the first time I saw her laugh since my little sister was stillborn. God bless the rain.

Back in the present, I am searching the sky for a cloud on a sweltering afternoon in London. Unfortunately, it is a clear blue sky and no chance of rain.

The Lady in the blue dress

Padua 1944

Emma, a courier in the resistance, never had any problems falling asleep before a mission. Her nerves of steel helped her stay calm in tricky situations; her calm demeanour gave credibility to any story she told when she was stopped at a roadblock or to check her documents. That mission was not particularly demanding; she had to deliver papers to an address in Verona and collect a downed airman and escort him to the next station on its way south to cross the frontline. Before falling asleep, she wondered about the cover story for her journey. Not long before waking up, she dreamt she was walking in a park; an old lady dressed in an old-fashioned blue dress stopped her and told her she should travel later in the day; there would be an air raid in Verona around 11 am.

The old lady in blue reminded Emma of one of her aunts, except her dress was from the mid-nineteenth century. Something in her voice and demeanour made Emma take that warning seriously, she decided to travel in the afternoon. She would simply say she had missed the train. The plans usually had flexibility, allied air raids were frequent in Northern Italy, and they would disrupt travel.

She and her sister Diana were discussing how to take a dress apart to make a jacket; Diana looked at the clock.

"Your old lady has ten minutes to be right; otherwise, I'll tease you for the rest of our lives."

She barely finished the sentence when they heard the noise of planes; they both rushed to the window and saw several bombers flying west in the direction of Verona. "Emma's old lady" had been right.

Venice, 1953

Emma had given birth to her second son. Unfortunately, there were a lot of issues, and several operations were required to give the baby the chance of a normal life. Emma and her husband were devastated. A week after giving birth, Emma was still spending most of her days crying. One night, she dreamt she was sitting on a bench in the Giardini of the Biennale, looking at the lagoon; it was a sunny day in the summer. Emma was there with her new-born son asleep in the pram. The old lady wearing a blue dress and lace gloves appeared, coming from the direction of the Lido. She stopped, looked at the baby, picked him up, kissed him on the forehead, put it back down, sat beside Emma, and held her hands.

"You must stop crying. Yes, your son will have operations, and your son will have problems, but your son will be stubborn enough to lead a successful life. He will excel in sports, get married, and have children. Your son is a fighter, and he will win"

Emma woke up strangely calm and rested; she got up and fed her son. While she was changing him, she told him about her dream. A two-week-old baby could not respond, but that son grew up listening to that story every time he had problems, and every time he was successful. Eighteen years later, when Gabriel came home excited because he had been selected for the Italian Olympic Swimming Team, Emma reminded him of her dream when he was two weeks old. The Old Lady had been right.

Venice 2021

Emma dreamt about "her old lady" several times. She was always wearing a blue and white dress with white gloves; the season would dictate whether the gloves were lace or leather. Her son Gabriel was fascinated by this person and wondered whether he could ever possibly dream about her. He loved the idea of somebody who would appear in his dreams to warn him or reassure him. Emma had always been adamant that "her old lady" had never been wrong.

The old lady visited Emma's dreams in November 2021. Emma was almost 98; she was not feeling well at all. She was in a lot of pain. When Gabriel visited her, she told him that "her old lady" had told her that everything would be all right. She had nothing to worry about. Emma was not afraid of dying; her old lady had reassured her.

Emma passed away on New Year's Eve. Gabriel was at home in London; his aunt called him when he was getting ready to go to his synagogue Friday night service.

London February 2022

His mother's old lady was the last thing in Gabriel's mind for the following month. He had too many things occupying the "forefront of his thoughts": sorting out his mother's home in Italy, the notes from the editor of his last book, the new novel he was writing, his eldest son in Israel, the mental health of his youngest daughter (a nurse in not yet post-pandemic London), and his own health issues. Sleep was not his friend. He kept waking up mentally exhausted; one night, he dreamt he was walking along Greenwich Park, something he had not done for decades. He decided to sit on the grass and look at Canary Wharf on the other side of the river when two ladies approached him; one was his mother, looking like she looked in her fifties, wearing the dress she wore at Gabriel's eldest son's bar mitzvah; the other was an old lady wearing a blue dress from the mid-nineteenth century and lace gloves. They were walking toward him, talking to each other. When they reached Gabriel, his mother told him off for sitting on the grass when there was a bench nearby. The old lady looked at Gabriel, smiling.

"Daniel will be fine; he will meet his soulmate in a few months. You shouldn't worry about Blanche; she can cope with the stress; she is your mother's granddaughter. Don't worry; your mother has asked me to follow your life from now on."

Gabriel's son Daniel really met his soulmate a few weeks after that dream.

Trieste, April 2022

Gabriel dreamt of the old lady another time when he was concerned about how long it would take to settle his mother's estate. The old lady reassured him but also told him to watch out for a few possible sources of delays or complications. Gabriel paid attention, and he was happy he did.

Gabriel's new book was a historical novel inspired by his great-grand-parents who met in Vienna in the 1860s. He got in touch with an older second cousin, the keeper of the family's papers.

The day after he arrived in Trieste, Gabriel went to his cousin's home to look for old letters in the family archives. They were in the study, looking at a box of letters; apparently, their great-grandmother was corresponding with her mother in Ladino, the language close to medieval Spanish spoken by many Jews in the Ottoman empire. He was reading a letter his great-grandmother wrote when she was expecting her first child. She praised her mother-in-law's ability to reassure her; Gabriel read aloud a sentence.

"It is almost as if she knows how I feel; her voice is so convincing that one is almost inclined to think that she knows the future."

Gabriel's cousin smiled and told him to look up. Gabriel looked at the painting behind his cousin as his cousin added

"Meet our great-great-grandmother, Stella Morpurgo, born Stella Basevi; she is the one whose voice made you think she knew the future."

Gabriel's looked up at a portrait of an elderly lady, probably painted after the 1860s. She was wearing a blue dress and lace gloves; she was walking in a garden holding a white parasol.

Gabriel froze; he was looking at the "old lady" of his dreams and probably the same old lady in his mother's dreams.

Gabriel's face must have turned white. His cousin asked him why. Gabriel told him that he had no memory of seeing that painting before, at least no rational memory. Then he proceeded to share his dreams of "His mother's old lady" with his cousins. His cousin smiled

"I am pretty sure you never saw the painting. My grandfather, your grandmother's brother, was the eldest male child, the son and heir to the name. He was fond of his grandmother, so when she died, he asked his parents if he could take the painting. I got it ten years ago when my mother passed away. You had no reason to be in my parents' bedroom. By the way, you are not the only family member dreaming of great-great-grandma. Stella Basevi Morpurgo comes into my dreams whenever I am stressed. I wonder who else she visits."

Transplanted roots

Roy was sipping coffee in the terrace; he was packed and ready to go. His suitcase and old laptop bag were waiting by the door, travelling companions of many trips. He had half an hour before the taxi arrived to take him to the airport. He was not ready for this trip. Rationally, he knew that the day would come; emotionally, his mother's death was an event he knew would happen sometimes in the future. Well, the future had arrived.

Two nights earlier he had woken up around 3am with the strong perception that his mother was in his bedroom telling him to wake up. He could hear her voice in his sleep, exactly like he had during his childhood and teen-age years, his mother had come to wake him up. A widower in his late sixties with four grown-up children he did not need to be woken up in time to go to school. He remembered sitting on the bed for quite some time, thinking of that strange dream. He was confident his mother had walked into his current bedroom; he did not dream about his bedroom when he was a teenager. He was unusually alert for three in the morning. Frank Sinatra's My Way, the ringtone of his mobile phone, stopped his train of thought. The photo of his eldest child Gabriel when he was six months, brought him back to reality. He remembered that Gabriel was visiting his grandmother with his husband and their set of twins. Why on earth was he ringing him at 8am his time? The penny dropped before he picked up the phone from the bedside table.

Roy's mother was 102, still in a good mental state. Gabriel and Reuven had taken care of the twins' morning routine. Once they sat at the breakfast table supervised by Reuven and Aunt Myriam, grandma's "baby sister", Gabriel had prepared coffee for the carer and mint tea for grandma. He went to wake her up carrying a tray with the tea and some biscuits. When he walked into her room, he realised she had passed away in her sleep. He was still in her room; he had not told the others yet.

Sipping coffee in the terrace, Roy was still wondering whether he had woken up the moment his mother was dying. He saw the taxi appear in the driveway, went back inside, put the mug in the dishwasher, grabbed his luggage, locked the door behind him and left for the airport.

Roy had managed to find a first-class ticket using frequent flyer points in one of the few remaining B747 flights. He had managed to book a seat in the first row, the one that almost gave him the same view as the pilot. He felt guilty to be so excited given why he was travelling. A frustrated pilot, he loved flying, even as a passenger. By the time the plane had reached cruise altitude he was back with his thoughts, the memories of his mother. Roy had an interesting relationship with his parents. After he left home for a life across the ocean, he decided to try to understand his parents. He thought about what he knew of their lives, talking to his aunts and his father's cousins. He tried to understand their choices and think of them as real people, not just mum and dad. Once he understood them, the relationship improved. By the time he had finished dinner he had congratulated himself for the relationship he had built with his father during the last ten years of his life. He had no regrets over the thirty-two years relationship he built with his widowed mother. The only child left after his older brother died at the age of eight, he had been lucky enough to have parents that supported him and his need to get on with his life. He had moved across the Atlantic, but he felt he had always been a presence. He had been lucky enough to have had the opportunity of stealing long weekends with his parents during business trips, took his children to see them at least twice a year. His finances suffered, but his family life did not. His mother had a real relationship with her four grandchildren when they were growing up, even with the older ones who were children when video calls were not a normal everyday occurrence. He finished dinner and tried to catch some sleep, in full knowledge that it was too early for him. He turned his seat in the bed position, changed into the pyjama provided by the airline, and closed his eyes. Sleep was elusive, he surprised himself thinking of the time when his first name was not Roy. He was named after an honorary great uncle much loved by his father. He had memories of his uncle Ranieri, a great storyteller who could keep him interested, and quiet, for hours when he was very young. Still, he hated being called Ranieri, he much preferred his Hebrew name Raphael and was eternally grateful to his maternal grandparents who called him Raphael, the Hebrew name of his maternal grandfather.

When he was 11, his paternal grandparents and an aunt, one of his father's sisters, had moved in. His 68 years old self knew very well it had not been an easy decision, his mother had a better relationship with her in-laws than his father had with his parents. The single aunt came as a package and his mother had managed an acceptable relationship with a sister-in-law who looked down on her. Still, his father had never forgiven his sister for things that happened during World War II and immediately after. The household was peaceful most days, except sometimes his father would explode and start a fight with his sister. They inevitably mentioned what happened during World War II before they fled to Switzerland. His grandparents had a very strong bond, but their relationship was based on constant bickering. In other words, it was more "blitzkrieg" than "peace in our time". Roy clearly remembered the time he was standing in front of the bathroom mirror, not yet thirteen, contemplating whether the stubbles he saw could be considered beard he ought to shave. He stood there one Sunday morning listening to the umpteenth battle erupting outside. He decided that he had to "transplant" himself somewhere else for his mental sanity. He decided that after his barmitzvah he would ask his friends to call him Raphael. His Jewish friends and his cousins would think it was a bit weird. He would tell his non-Jewish friends that it was a family tradition, a way to mark the transition to adulthood; they would not know better. When he met Sharon, an American medical student in Padua, she started calling him Roy and he liked Roy. He was so in love with her that he would probably have loved whatever name she would have used for him, but Roy stuck. Roy had become the name everybody used. His mother was not enthusiastic at the beginning but after his father passed away, she slowly accepted it. Ranieri was a name she was using when they were reminiscing about his childhood, they were talking about Ranieri almost as if he had been somebody else. He had been somebody else. Roy was more confident, less anxious, and less impulsive. Ranieri was bullied, Roy was popular.

Sleep was not coming. According to his internal clock, his regular bedtime was supposed to be when the plane would be starting its approach to Frankfurt airport, by then he had to be awake. Roy's mind was retrieving childhood memories of his parents. He had a lot of happy memories, mostly tied to whenever his parents were at peace with themselves. Nowadays people would say they had PTSD, then he only knew that both parents had gone through very tough times. He remembered a car journey somewhere in the Alps, his father singing along a Frank Sinatra song from the car radio, his mother swaying sideways with the rhythm. It was "their song", he could see from the rear view mirror his father smiling and he could guess that his mother was smiling too. His mother loved music but never sung. She was just humming along. If he remembered correctly, his brother was not with them. That meant Ranieri was at least five, Michael died when he was eight and Ranieri was four. He used to talk about his childhood memories as if they were somebody else's. They were Ranieri's memories, he was Roy. He only used the first person to say that he hated his name when he was a child.

As predicted, he was feeling sleepy when they served breakfast. One of the luxuries of first-class travel was the availability of espresso coffee, so much better than the regular coffee available on board. He asked for it twice, he needed it to stay awake. Being met at the plane with a car that would drive him to the First-Class lounge was the other luxury perk associated with transit as a first-class passenger; he avoided the enormous labyrinth that is Frankfurt airport.

By the time he boarded the flight to Venice he realised that Roy could tell his twelve years old self that he had managed to "transplant" himself; Roy's roots were firmly in his maternal grandmother's family. The only thing he had in common with his paternal relatives was a distinctive Italian Jewish last name that had a lot of history in Northern Italy but was completely unknown anywhere else. During the short flight he realised that he had spent hours in Ranieri's memory lane. He had not revisited any memory he had of his mother when he was an adult, and there were many. It was only when he was on the waterbus to Venice that he realised that he was grieving two people, his mother and Ranieri. His Aunt Myriam was the only person left who knew who Ranieri was, although they never talked about his childhood. His mother was the link between Roy and Ranieri. Now, the link was gone. The transplanted roots were very strong. After the funeral, he had to visit his father's grave to reassure him once again that Roy was still his child.

Dancing in my head

When I was a teenager in north-eastern Italy, I belonged to a dancing group. We were doing what in that part of Italy, in those days was called "Viennese dancing". If you have ever watched the New Year Concert from Vienna the dancing included in the television concerts is a more ballet-like version of what we were doing.

Think of Viennese Waltzes, Polka, Mazurka, Quadrille, rather than fox-trot, quick-steps, waltzes. We had couple dances, small group dances and large group dances.

So, I am at my desk facing a window overlooking the Thames, working at my second novel. I am listening to Strauss on Spotify the 'Emperor Waltz' (KaiserWaltzer) starts and my mind goes to one particular time when we were dancing it as a group of eight couples. The classic Emperor waltz has an introduction of about 2 minutes. We had 2 minutes for our choreographed entrance as a group.

We are 'in position' a few minutes before going in. Four couples from the middle of each side of the rectangular shaped dance floor, four couples placed at the corners. We have rehearsed for weeks; so, it is down to muscle memory, not counting. Our *Tanzmeister* (Dance Captain) checks that we have the correct position, relaxed shoulders and rigid, straight back. One should be able to draw a perfectly straight line starting from the middle of the top of our head down to the centre point of the space between our feet. My right hand is on the left hand of my dancing partner, the palm of my hand slightly touching the back of her hand. The introduction start, 15 seconds later the Tanzmeister gives us a sign and we start moving. Young Men are wearing a black dinner jacket and the young women are wearing long flowing evening dresses that allow movement, we are all wearing blue and golden silk sashes simulating a sort of decoration. The idea is that we are going to an imaginary ball in an imaginary imperial palace. We have one minute to reach our positions, then another minute for my dancing partner to move in front of me. My right hand and her left hand do not move. I bow, she curtseys, and we assume the waltz position exactly in time with the end of the introduction. The waltz starts and we start waltzing. The eight couples make a circle half way inside the dance floor.

It is not just a memory; I hear the music and I re-live it in my head. I feel the same elation, the same sense of lightness, the fluidity of moving around the dance floor, I feel the happiness I used to feel when I was dancing...and this old man with a prosthetic leg and a very bad back is dancing... is dancing in his head.

The quintet

Nobody could beat them when they were ten. They were so in tune with each other, so able to communicate with a nod or a gesture that they did not need to shout like the other children playing basket, or cricket, in the school yard. Of course, they were a team. They had been spending most of their time together since they were three, three of them could hardly remember when they met. Mahesh, Jomo, and Daniel were less than a year when their mothers put them in the same playpen for the first time.

They were now in their sixties and Mahesh, Jomo, Daniel, Jean-Francois, and Max could still communicate with a look or a gesture, except they were not playing basket that morning. They had just arrived from the resort on the shores of the Indian ocean after what they feared was the last time they had an outing all together, just them, no family.

Geography did not defeat their bond, during their lives they lived in many different places, but they all managed to meet for a week every other year. They also managed to be present at important times in the other ones' lives. The last time was five years earlier, before the pandemic, when Mahesh youngest daughter got married in California. They were at the wedding with all their families, their children referring to each other as honorary cousins.

This time was a different important moment for one of them, Jomo had his first chemo session. They all had to be there, they had arrived at Nairobi from different parts of the world. They spent four days in Nialy Beach where they all grew up. On the fifth day they took the new Chinese built train to Nairobi. They kept cracking jokes and retrieving funny memories all the way to the clinic. By the time Jomo was checked in he was in good spirits; a very bossy nurse stopped Daniel, Mahesh, Jean-Francois, and Max from going in saying it was families only.

Jomo's eldest son, George, who had met them at the clinic, intervened

"They are all my uncles!"

The nurse looked at him, then looked at Jomo and at each one of the other four. Jomo was half kikuyu, half Masai, Mahesh was Indian, Jean-Francois was a blond blue-eyed Frenchman and Daniel and Max were white Jews.

"Uncles?" – said the nurse with an annoyed look

"I didn't say they had the same mother" said George smiling.

At the end the Kenyan version of Nurse Ratchet relented and simply said

"One uncle at a time!"

Jean-Francois went first, the other sat in the waiting room contemplating their own mortality. George gave up trying to make conversation. After twenty minutes of silence, Mahesh smiled. The other three raised their eyebrows, so he felt he had to explain

"Do you remember the first day of school, when we caught the school bus for the first time?"

Nyaly Beach, Mombasa, Kenya, September 1959

Five boys are ready for the first day of school. They all wear their uniforms, tan shorts, white shirts, brown jacket and brown rider cap. Some serendipitous alignment of whatever was supposed to align meant that they are all going to the same school. Daniel, Max, Jean Francois, Mahesh and Jomo will be in the same form. The gang of five will not be broken.

They are waiting for the school bus with Max's older sister. Susan tells them that the uniform will be too warm later in the day when the African sun will show its full force. Nine year's old Susan is four years older – and forty years wiser – than the gang of five. The gang of five is a mixed bunch, Daniel is Italian and his father works for an oil company, Jean Francois is French and his father works for a shipping company, Max is American and his father works at the US consulate in Mombasa, Mahesh was born in Kenya and is the son of an accountant and Jomo was born in Kenya and is the son of a doctor. It is before the East African Independence Act, Kenya was definitely a colony.

The bus arrives. The children sit in pairs. Max and his sister, Jean Francois and Jomo, Daniel and Mahesh. They wave at their parents who wave back. Finally the bus moves.

At the next bus stop a friend of Susan's gets on and Max's sister moves to sit near her. The driver reminds them that they should not change seats when the bus is moving. Max now is standing on his knees in his seat, turned back towards his friends. The driver from time to time shouts "Hey you, what's your name, sit down!", Max ignores him.

The bus now reaches the very wealthy part of Nialy Beach. Three boys get on. Susan from the other side of the aisle whisper to her brother "Here comes trouble". The older of the three - a tall red haired boy – stands by Jomo and tells him to move because he wants to sit in the shade. The driver has come to check what's going on. Apparently the red haired boy is a known trouble maker. The driver stands next to

Jomo and whispers "mzungu", a Swahili word for white man. Jean Francois looks at Daniel, Max and Mahesh, then says "Why don't we all sit in the back there are five seats next to each other". Susan goes back to her friend. The driver smiles, the gang of five moves to the back of the bus.

Max smiles, stands up to get some water. Daniel puts down the magazine he had not opened yet and sits upright

"We sat on those seats every school days for seven years. They became our seats, nobody else ever tried to sit there."

Max comes back with four paper cups of water balanced on the book he was pretending to read. Mahesh picks one, and

"Jean-Francois was a great diplomat even then. Do we remember who was the tall red haired boy who always caused trouble?"

George always loved listening to his father and his uncles talk about their memories. He wished he had developed the same type of close bonds with friends, sadly it never happened. He was most definitely not in touch with the friends of his pre-school year and he was thirty years younger than the quintet. This time, he thinks he has the answer.

"If I remember correctly, he used to be the son of the judge that replaced my great-grandfather, dad told me once that he remembers he was at the retirement ceremony when my great-grandfather retired."

Max throws the empty cup in the bin

"I did not lose my aim...we were at the same ceremony but I do not remember him and Babu[1] George introduced all five of us as his grandchildren. I remember it very well."

"Maybe we do not remember him because we never liked him. Jomo might have had other opportunities to see him."

George was in a position to fill the blanks

"Uncle Daniel, if he is the person I think he is , he is still in Kenya. Somehow dad invited him to his retirement party when he stepped off the bench."

The lift doors opened and Jean-Francois appeared. He spoke directly to the receptionist

"The doctors upstairs told me to tell you that you can send up two at a time. You can call the nurse station to check if you do not believe me."

Mahesh and George went upstairs. Jean-Francois sat down

"What did I miss?"

"Nothing much, we sat in silence for a while then we started talking of our first trip on the school bus, how is Judge Jomo?"

They started calling him Judge Jomo quite a few years earlier, when they were in the States when Mahesh eldest son got married. One of the other guests to the wedding pointed out that "Judge Jomo" sounded almost as good as "Judge Judy", and after all Jomo was a judge. It was all the incentive they needed, from that moment on they always referred to him as Judge Jomo.

Could an object represent your roots?

In January 2022, when I was clearing up my mother's home, I wondered whether it was worth my while to take my mother's dining room table to London. The table dates back to 1921; in 2022, it is considered an antique. I liked my modern living room, all white with paintings, cushions and armchairs bringing in colour. How would an antique piece of furniture fit in that room?

Yet, my mother's table stayed in my mind. An only child, I had nobody with whom I had to share my mother's belongings, so I had been bringing small things to London for quite some time. In 2017 a stroke forced my mother's move to a nursing home; since then, I have been flying to Italy once a month to see her. Each time, I left London with one suitcase and a bag that could be folded into a small purse and would check in two pieces of luggage on my way back. I successfully brought home glasses, plates, paintings, and other objects I loved. My close friends and family teased me over my ability to pack anything in my luggage and get it to London in one piece.

By the time my mother passed away on the last day of 2021, I had already taken to London most objects that meant a lot to me and could fit either in my suitcase or my bag. I was playing with the idea of organising something to bring larger family pieces to London. The dining room table was not part of it, yet I was drawn to it. I kept dithering during the whole month of January. Talking about it to my eldest son, I realised I hated the idea of "that table" in some stranger's living room. So, I decided to take it to London.

Every morning I am thrilled to see it there. It had come home. That table had been in my family for three generations. My grandparents married in 1921; that was their original dining room table. When we moved back to Italy in 1966, my grandparents gave it to my parents; in 2022, that table is in my home.

My hydroponics roots are not connected to one specific place; they are more tied to cultural influences and the influence of previous generations. That table represents a sense of continuity. A lot of memories are centred around it: eating Friday night dinners and huge family meals during Jewish holidays in my grandparents' home when I was a child, birthday dinners with friends when I was a teenager, my father sitting at the head of the table when we had guests, me freaking out when an aunt told me to sit at the head of the table when we came back from my father's funeral.

In my grandparents' home, my grandfather's seat at that table faced a window, and so did my father's in my parents' home. I had guests for the first time since I had "the table" in my home; I sat in the most convenient place to get to the kitchen. When I sat down, I realised my seat was facing the window. It is as if I had received the baton my grandfather passed on to his eldest daughter. I had to have that table in my home because it was a place where my hydroponic roots could rest.

Shirley and Nancy

A tall African woman will always represent 'Mother Earth' to me. Nancy was my nanny in Kenya, the woman who looked after my mother and me for three years when my mother was not feeling well. I was three when I met Nancy, and since then, I always feel safe when a tall African woman is in charge. It is not just the look but also the voice, the smile, and the accent.

Caroline and I are about to have a child, following many attempts that resulted in a miscarriage. We can relax now; it will not even be a premature baby. Our child is due tomorrow. However, the child is not born yet. We are nervous because things can go wrong. It happened four years ago, and the fear it may happen again is palpable. Caroline and I never discuss it, but it is not the proverbial elephant in the room. It is a herd of elephants in the room.

Caroline insists I go to work; she says she is fine. I reluctantly go; I do everything Caroline tells me to do this week. She needs to be calm, as calm as she can possibly be. In reality, she is far from calm. She is with our herd of elephants the whole day; I leave them at the door of my office.

Sometimes in the afternoon, Caroline rings me in tears.

"Grandma is here, and we wanted to take a walk in the park; I cannot lock the back door; I feel so stupid. Can you come home?"

My boss was in my office and heard my side of the phone call, a father of four he tells me to go home. I do not know why, but he thinks Caroline has started labour; he even calls the company car service to organise a car to take me home. I get in the car, and about half an hour later, we are outside my home; the driver wishes me good luck. I get off the car and walk into the playpen of the herd of elephants.

Caroline's grandmother greets me.

"She is sitting down; I think labour has started."

I dare ask whether she is sure; her tone of voice almost makes me regret I asked.

"I had five children; don't you think I can recognise a woman in labour?"

Caroline comes out of our sitting room.

"I am so happy to see you; thank you for coming home."

My wife is not prone to public displays of affection, verbal or otherwise. Now I am really worried. I wish I could find my inner steel core so I could calmly reassure her, but it seems to be temporarily unavailable.

"Do you think we ought to go to the hospital?"

Caroline looks at me, then looks at her grandmother, who has no doubt.

"You look like a woman in labour. Go as fast as you can."

Driving fast when your passenger is a pregnant woman about to give birth ... easier said than done! All I can think about is holding Samuel before he gave his last breath four years earlier; he only lived six hours. Caroline never held him alive.

I am surprised we reached the hospital without any problem. Caroline refuses the wheelchair; a contraction makes her change her mind. At the maternity ward, they looked surprised; they weren't expecting us until the following day at best. However, her waters break as the doctor examines her. There is no question she is in labour. They are not sending us home; we are assigned a midwife.

The midwife is a big woman who speaks English with a strong Swahili accent. She takes us to the room where Caroline will be till our baby is born. Our midwife is a tall, imposing lady with broad shoulders and a smile that can light up a room. I am immediately transported to my childhood and Nancy. I even think she has the same voice; honestly, I cannot say whether that is the case or I just hear her speaking with Nancy's voice. What I hear is her reassuring Caroline in the same way that Nancy used to reassure my mother. The words and the circumstances may differ, but the tone of voice is similar.

I don't know how Shirley's words affect Caroline, but she has stopped crying. We have our equivalent of Nancy; our daughter was born half an hour before the end of Shirley's shift.

Shirley had managed to calm down a very distressed mother, just like Nancy used to do with mine. I knew it the moment I saw her. Just looking at her, hearing her talk in that tone, with that voice, made me think of the person that had meant stability, control and calmness for three years of my life. The person that enabled my mother to be all those things for the rest of my childhood. Everything was great when Nancy was around, and I am sure everything turned out to be all right because Shirley was around.

Roy's first flight

The American grandparents insist on having their latest grandchild for his first Thanksgiving. The parents are not so keen; they keep making excuses. The Italian grandparents clearly are members of the 'Great grandparents conspiracy' and insist that flying with a baby is not a problem. The father flew for the first time when he was six months old, and by the time he turned one, he had already flown three times long-haul, and that happened twenty-three years earlier. When the paediatrician confirms there are no problems, the parents have no choice. The American grandparents send the tickets.

Ruth and I found ourselves starting our first long haul flight with our six-month-old son one fine November morning in 1976. We are young and hopeless; at least, that is what my mother and grandmother think. We are anxious new parents, so we have packed everything, including spare nappies (or diapers as they call them in the US) and a travel cot; we have a massive suitcase for the baby and one for the two of us. In those days, "a lady's handbag" was not considered part of the 'hand luggage' (as it was called then), so Ruth carried a handbag that could easily fit a Venetian waterbus with room to spare.

The result is akin to an expedition of a nineteenth century African explorer. My mother decides to take the morning off work to come with us to the airport to help. My very practical grandmother rings for porters to help us get to the stop of the waterbus to the airport. My mother also acts as a decoy; three adults, a baby and three suitcases look less pathetic than a very nervous couple of young parents with a baby and all that luggage.

We arrive at the airport; we fly to London, where we will take a connecting flight to Washington, DC. My mother keeps saying that twenty-three years earlier, things were different. She keeps saying it to everybody. I was the baby she kept talking about; now I am a young twenty-three-year-old father trying to look competent rather than very embarrassed; after all, I am a pilot, a first officer flying 727s. My mother's embarrassing tales succeed in getting us some help. We can use all the help we can get considering that we carry on board the following: a bag that would fit under the seat with a change of clothes for the baby and a change of tops for the parents, a 'baby bag' with nappies, food for the babies and other relevant things (does not count as 'hand luggage' as well), Ruth's mega handbag (does not count) and Ruth's hand luggage... and a six months old baby. My mother was great at getting crew members to help her, but we were not as good.

We followed my mother's advice and gave Roy something to suck during take-off so his ears did not hurt and he behaved. Roy is fascinated by the various lights he sees. At six months, he was not afraid of strangers. A Venetian baby, he was used to strangers approaching the pram and trying to make him smile, so he now smiles at everybody, winning over the flight crew. Italian flight attendants ask to hold our pretty little boy for a while so that the parents can eat. Not sure who is doing a favour to whom.

One of my father-in-law's closest friends was the military attaché to the US embassy in London. He managed to pull some strings and meet us at the gate when we arrived, officially, to help, but in reality, he wanted to see the baby and 'inspect' the father. He could not make it to the wedding. After all these years, I am still not sure whether I felt intimidated or a VIP when I saw two men in a US Navy uniform meeting us at the gate. I had heard of 'Uncle Harry' before but had never met him, and I most definitely did not expect to meet him at Heathrow. In any case, the younger officer is ordered to help us. We have our own Sherpa!

Shamelessly, Ruth gives him the heaviest bags, so a 'convoy' changes terminals at Heathrow. 'Uncle Harry' holding Roy with Ruth by his side, followed by myself with two bags and the 'Sherpa,' i.e. the young US Navy officer with two heavy bags. Our honorary uncle had pulled strings to make us transfer in a mini-bus rather than the regular transfer bus normal people use. Uncle Harry managed to organise access to the Pan Am lounge. 'Uncle Harry' now interviews me while Ruth feeds the baby. I still do not know whether I passed or not. Our "escorts" take us to the plane. When we were about to leave the lounge, the receptionist gave us two new boarding cards. Roy and his parents had been upgraded to First Class!

We board the plane to the astonishment of the other passengers in First Class. After take-off, I hold the baby, and Ruth has lunch; while she eats, I change Roy. Then Ruth takes the baby for a walk across the plane, and I eat. Our son is remarkably quiet. With impeccable timing, he falls asleep in his cot. We are careful not to move for fear of waking him up; "let sleeping dogs lie" also applies to babies.

Ruth and I are full of parental pride when the flight crew and other passengers tell us how great our son is; so far, he did not cry. Until we had to wake him up for landing, and he complained. Luckily he thought the seat belt was a new toy, and he was fascinated by the extension, so he stopped crying. US citizens born abroad must go through the alien line when entering the US for the first time. We all went through the alien line as a family group to simplify things, Ruth tried it for the first time and did not like the experience.

Ruth's parents were outside waiting for us; I am sure they were waiting for their grandson, and we were just part of the package. They insisted on taking a photo of us, two sleep-deprived and slightly dishevelled adults and one smiling baby. Roy still has that photo in his living room.

New York State of Mind

Forty years ago, Ruth and I had a week of interviews in New York at the end of October. Ruth was interviewing at Mount Sinai hospital, and I had a second interview with a financial technology consultancy in the Wall Street Area. We decided to take our son Roy with us. We landed in a relatively warm and sunny New York. One of Ruth's brothers had suggested a Hotel in the upper west side that was renting apartments by the day. We booked a two-bedroom place for a week. It was near Central Park.

At three and a half, Roy was a veteran of long-haul flights, just like I had been twenty-three years earlier. He had been to the US several times, but it was his first time in New York. He was expecting the George Washington Parkway, the motorway in the woods that was the first section of the journey from Washington National Airport (now Ronald Regan airport) to his uncle's place on the Maryland side of suburban Washington. He was also used to a suburban environment with large gardens (or 'yards' as they call them in the US) and many trees. He was surprised by the urban landscape of Queens and Brooklyn. He was on my lap when we were driving to

Manhattan from the airport, and he was not sure where we were; once the taxi entered Central Park, he turned to me and said, "Now I recognise the United States!"

He loved Central Park. When his American grandmother arrived to babysit for us, he would ask to go to Central Park. When we moved to New York, he always wanted a 'Chinese picnic' in the park. His second love was the Staten Island ferry. One day when Ruth was busy and I was not, I had to take four trips to Staten Island (as in there and back four times). We were surprised that he was happy to return to Venice at the end of the week in New York. We thought he was excited about the flight, but eight years later, I discovered that he thought that Venice was his safe place, away from the nightmares that his mother's death had given him.

We shamelessly used Ruth's mother during the four days she spent with us. We were out every night and even took a carriage ride in Central Park in the dark.

At the end of the week, we were on a plane back to Venice with two job offers to start the following January.

Despite what happened eight years later, after forty years, I have very nice memories, a lot of them, and I love the city. During the lockdown, I dreamt of walking in Central Park, getting a Chinese takeaway, or going to the theatre. New York has a way of getting into your bones after a while.

Memories of Christmas past

I always had a funny relationship with Christmas. As a Jewish child, it was somebody else's holiday, the reason why I was off school for a few days. In the past few years, as a divorced man with four grown-up children, it has been a reason to chill out for two days, read a book, listen to music, watch cheesy movies, put my brain on a shelf (metaphorically speaking), and just relax. Then came COVID and lockdown. Living alone, I could "chill" every weekend, so I did not expect it to be a big deal. It turned out I could not have been more wrong.

In December 2020, friends decided to throw a Zoom Christmas party. Guests were divided into break-out rooms every twenty minutes; it was a way to mingle. People volunteered to entertain everybody between one twenty-minute slot and another. During one of those breaks, a friend read "it was a night before Christmas", a poem by Clement Clarke Moore; her Jewish father used to read it to her at Christmas. That brought back memory of Christmas in New York.

Many moons ago, in the 1980s, I lived in New York with my wife, Ruth, and my son, Roy (Reuven). Ruth was a doctor and used to take the Christmas shifts; it was not our holiday, after all. Christmas became a father-and-son affair. I used to travel a lot, and I came to treasure those three days with my son.

The alarm sounded at 6.30 like any other workday. Ruth would go in the shower; I would go into the kitchen to make her breakfast. Those thirty minutes in the morning were our time. Our conversation was always a mixture of very personal and very pragmatic, like every couple of working parents who spend most of their day apart. At 730, Ruth would leave for her shift; since it was winter, a Taxi would take her across the park to her hospital. Roy was still asleep; I usually went back to bed.

At some point in the morning, Roy knocked at my door. He knew he should not barge into his parents' bedroom. I would always answer with a sleepy voice, whether I had gone back to sleep or simply stayed in bed reading. Roy's way to start Christmas was to catapult himself onto my bed, sit on his knees next to me and begin reciting the poem " 'Twas the night before Christmas"; he had learnt it during his first year in school. He thought Christmas morning was perfect for the poem because the home was silent when he woke up. He related it to "not a creature was stirring, not even a mouse". By the time the poem ended, I had pulled myself up, sitting on the bed next to him, waiting for the hug I knew I would get. Much to my annoyance, my father, his Italian grandfather, had taught him to say "Christmas Sameach", inspired by "Chag Sameach" (Happy Holiday), the greeting Jews exchange on holidays. I did not like mixing things, my father thought that Christmas had minimal religious content left, so it wasn't really "mixing things". After the hug, we would get up, and "we" would make breakfast. Usually, I would make blueberry pancakes while he ate his cereals at the breakfast bar. It was the first conversation of the day. We talked about my last business trip and shared some blueberry pancakes when I supervised his breakfast. Over time, Roy would find a way to read something associated with the place where I had been (with the help of his school librarian), and we would talk about the city, how much I'd seen of it, my journey there and back, my jet lag, etc.

The conversation would continue as I supervised him brushing his teeth, washing his face, and getting dressed. He would then watch cartoons on TV while I showered and got dressed. When I reappeared, he would tell me about what he had just seen. Then we would go out. Our first destination was Central Park, half a block from our Upper West Side home. Depending on how late it was, we would spend some time watching the skaters or just walking around the park discussing whatever was happening in his life, usually school.

Our winter walks in Central Park usually allowed us to have "meaningful" father-son conversations. Roy was born in Venice; he was three when we moved to New York, and we would take him back at least once a year. My parents would keep him there for a month each summer. It was his parents' "holiday time". Roy and I considered ourselves Venetian and loved being near the water. He used to say that "water made him think" (He is in his forties now; he still does say that!). We used to spend a significant amount of time by the lake when we were in Central Park.

We usually ended up on the other side of the park, where I would ring the Mount Sinai hospital ward nurse station where Ruth was working. If Ruth was not busy with an emergency, we would go to say hello. We would wait for her at the nurse station, where the nurses would give Roy a piece of cake (and maybe more when I was not looking), waiting for Ruth to come and say hello to us. She would take him to say "Merry Christmas" to some patients she thought were lonely. Half an hour later, we would leave the hospital, cross the park, and go and get the Christmas lunch we had booked from the Kosher Chinese takeaway on West 72nd and Columbus. Along the way, Roy would comment on the decorations of the shops. He loved a gigantic candy cane that used to hang outside the shop of the local dry cleaner on Columbus Avenue; he used to stand under it to see how much he had grown (he stopped when he was 10, by then, he was too tall to fit under the candy cane). We would then go home, put away whatever we would have for dinner with Ruth and eat lunch.

If breakfast was Roy asking about me, lunch was me asking him to talk about himself; It was a conversation interrupted by

"Please pass the fried rice."

Or

"Is there any cashew chicken left?"

We had shared interests in films and music, and often we ended up discussing which musical he wanted to see and when I could take him to see it. We both got a kick out of speaking different languages. Our lunchtime conversations were seldom dull or forced.

Once we had cleared lunch, if the weather was nice, we might meet some other families from our synagogue in Central Park. If it was raining and we had no play date, we would watch a film or listen to music we both liked while reading a book. We could share the same space while doing our things, and we still can; it was, and it is very nice.

Unless there were emergencies, Ruth would be home by 6. She would change into tracksuits, and we would have dinner. After dinner, Roy was sent to bed because mummy and daddy needed their time together.

Our "father and son Christmas" dramatically changed after Ruth died in a car accident, leaving me a widower with an 11-year-old and a six-month-old, the brother Roy always wanted. Now I live in London, and Roy lives in Tel Avi; I am 68, and Roy is 43. His brother, Jonathan, lives in Haifa. We Facetime at least once a week and message each other whenever something happens.

After the Zoom Christmas Party, I sent him a WhatsApp message saying that somebody had read " 'Twas the night before Christmas" to everybody participating in a Zoom call. The only comment I received back was, "How sweet". A week later, on Christmas day, the phone wakes me up at 830am, a very sleepy hello is met by Roy's voice saying, " 'Twas a night before Christmas, when all through the house, not a creature was stirring, not even a mouse..."[1]. Roy had picked up a tradition after a 33-year hiatus! By the time he got to the names of Santa's reindeers, I was in floods of tears.

When I heard Jonathan's voice saying, "love you, dad, but I am at work" (December 25th is not a holiday in Israel), I realised that Roy was trying to include his younger brother in what was the memory of a day just for the two of us.

In December 2020, Israel's borders were still closed to non-citizens and non-residents, and, thankfully, I did not have any urgent need to travel. Memories of Christmas in New York, relived together on a FaceTime call between London and Tel Aviv, a social distance-friendly way for a (Jewish) father and son team to be together on Christmas during COVID, alone but together.

[1] From " 'Twas the night before Christmas" by Clemens Clarke Moore

Princess Kilimanjaro

Kilimanjaro is an isolated mountain in the Rift Valley at the border between Kenya and Tanzania. Babu George ('Babu' means Grandpa in Swahili), my honorary African grandfather, told me the story of a Masai princess that had fallen in love with a Kikuyu farmer. The father of the princess did not like the idea of his daughter marrying a Kikuyu farmer, he forbade his daughter to see him ever again. The princess was in love and did not want to leave her farmer, so she turned herself into a mountain to be close to him. How do we know that the Kilimanjaro is the princess? Because she wears a necklace and a veil after she wakes up.

I was eight the first time I saw the mountain. It was a four days 'Safari' with my father to the Amboseli National Park, one of several 'father and son' trips ('Safari' in Swahili means journey. When I was a child living in Kenya, I used to go 'on Safari' to Venice four times a year). Approaching the park, I was more excited to see the mountain than the animals. I wanted to see the princess. The protagonist of several stories I heard from Babu George. Growing up in Africa does not mean that you see elephant, giraffes, lions, zebra, etc. every day.

They are very exotic to an urban African child. I knew the animals from photographs, the idea of seeing them in real life was exciting, but, to me, not as exciting as seeing the princess.

You need to wake up early in the morning to go on a drive to see animals. I saw the princess for the first time on my way to breakfast! Almost fifty-nine years later the image I have in my memory is slightly unrealistic, but I remember a very pink sky and the snow-capped top of the mountain looking pink. It was like Babu George had told us. The princess had not woken up yet! She was not wearing a veil or her necklace! It was a privilege to see her asleep.

When we came home from the drive the sun had already risen, again Babu George was right. There were clouds and you could still see the mountaintop but not as clearly as a couple of hours earlier before sunrise!

The king had ordered the sun to tell his daughter to wake up and get dressed, she was wearing her veil and her necklace!

Better than the most spectacular rock concert

You wake up at an unearthly hour in the morning to secure your seat, you cannot buy tickets in advance. You are surprised by the number of vehicles of all sorts that are on the road in the dark, all going to the ticket office. Tuk-tuks with young backpackers, luxury air-conditioned minibuses, or regular (air conditioned) car with a guide and tourists. Somehow the idea that the traffic at four am in the morning is all going to the same place is part of the excitement. There is a huge crowd waiting to buy tickets, two dozen very long lines of people. 24 counters open at the same time. The place is very noisy. People in the queue strike conversations, everybody is looking forward to the main event. They swap advice on the best place to go, where to find places to sit, what to do afterwards. The queue moves fast and sooner than you think you have the ticket!

You go back to your driver, and you are on your way. Once again on the road, all sort of vehicles heading for the same place. Soon you drive past two guards who check your tickets. The driver parks the car. Gives you two bottles of water and you and your guide are off to find the best place to sit with an unencumbered view.

You cross a very wide moat on a pontoon bridge, then you cross a gate straight from Indiana Jones and the temple of doom. You are surrounded by other people, all here for the main event.

Soon you reach a huge opening, with a lake in the middle and the stage for this main event reflecting on the water. There is light enough that you do not need torches. Your guide finds a huge rock where you can sit, somewhere where you can still see the stage and its reflection on the lake. The crowd is huge but not annoying, you are there for the same reason. You want to see the star of the show.

There is no screaming, shouting, not even a collective 'oooohhh', just a sense of excitement when the stage is back lit by an orange light. The star of the show is about to appear. Soon the reflection of the stage on the lake becomes clearer, the orange light more intense. You are ready with your phone to take a photo. You try not to get distracted by the image on the surface of the lake framed by water lilies. Then... the sun rises between the domes of the temple of Angkor Wat.

You realise that there is silence, and nobody moves. In your head, you can see the standing ovation and hear the roaring applause.

He is a fighter

December 1953

Deborah - Viola's sister who lived in Rome - had decided to follow her husband, who had a business trip to Bologna. Ada - Viola's sister who lived in Bologna - had decided to turn the occasion into the last opportunity for the three sisters to be together before giving birth. So, they convinced Viola to travel to Bologna from Venice; she was the one who was supposed to give birth last. The three sisters had been shopping for their future babies, everything white. It was the time before CT scans when the sex of the baby was a genuine surprise. Their father had predicted three sons, but that was because he wanted three grandsons. The three heavily pregnant women had come home and crashed in the sitting room, feet up and a mug of hot chocolate in their hands.

"Is Michael excited by the new brother or sister?" asked Ada. Michael was Viola's eldest child.

"Yes, although I am not sure whether he is excited for the new baby or excited because he knows that his dad will come to visit."

Answered Viola.

"And when are you planning to join Simon in Kenya?" asked Deborah

"Doctor Coin wrote a letter to a hospital in Mombasa, asking about weather conditions. He reckons that the best time for me to travel would be late June; by then, the baby will have experienced the humidity of Venice in June and will not find the climate in Mombasa very different, just a bit hotter."

"Will you fly or sail there?" asked Ada

"Of course, I'll fly. I can't think of anything worse than a week on a ship with a baby and five years old...."

Viola could not finish the sentence. Ada's mother-in-law came into the room and said that her husband was on the phone. Viola went to the hall, where a chair had been placed near the phone for her comfort. Her husband – Simon – did not leave her much time to talk after saying hello.

"I have planned everything to be there when the baby is born. I'll fly. How are you doing? How are Deborah and Ada?"

Viola started talking when something happened.

"Sorry, Simon, I do not think you'll be here in time. Your child seems as impatient as I am; the waters just broke. I need to go; bye."

Viola shouted; Ada's mother-in-law appeared, saw the puddle on the floor, hung up the phone and called an ambulance.

* * *

Almost forty hours later, a son was born with complications. There was something wrong with his hands and his right foot. Viola could barely look at him without crying. She felt like a total failure; one of her children was born with a heart problem that would make it unlikely that he would reach past puberty, and now this one had issues as well. She was told that nobody could have predicted what happened. Science had not figured out how Amniotic Band Syndrome – the name of the condition – developed and why. It was very rare and unlucky that it happened to her and her child.

In any way, her child could be described either as a miracle or as a fighter. At birth, they thought he was dead. Things were so serious for Viola that they were all focused on her until the baby started crying.

* * *

Simon made it to Bologna five days after the birth of his son. He had arrived straight from Rome after flying from Kenya, and he was afraid of flying! When he reached the hospital, Viola was crying.

"I look at him, and I feel like a failure."

"I look at him, and I see a fighter", replied Simon "we both fought back during the war; we shall fight to give him as normal a life as possible. He is our son, and we shall support him in his fight. I love him, and I love you."

"I love you too. How come you are here so early? You didn't fly, did you?" – Simon hated flying almost as strongly as Viola hated sea travel.

"As a matter of fact, I did. I had to wait two days for a flight to Rome and did not change my mind."

Viola stopped crying and started smiling.

"You are right; he is a fighter. We survived World War II; we'll get through this; we'll support him through this."

The lake of his dreams

Long ago, Paul dreamed of sitting on a terrace looking at a lake at the edge of a wood. Water, tall trees and mountains were all in his line of vision. In the distance, a seaplane was taking off. He associated that dream with a lake in Canada, not a specific lake. Each time he thought back to that scene, it reminded him of Canada.

The memory of that dream stayed with him for a long time. The first summer after his wife died, Paul left his sons with his grandmothers and took a road trip in the Alps by himself. He had no idea where to go; he just wanted to spend a few days alone. He loved his sons, but he needed the chance to grieve by himself seven months after the car accident that took his soulmate away from him and left his sons without a mother.

He rented a convertible, maybe because the first time he and Sharon took a road trip, his cousin lent him his MG. Anyway, he was looking forward to scenic drives. He had no idea where he would go, his only plan was to spend the first three days going somewhere and the second set of three days driving back to the beach where, by then, his parents and his in-laws would have spoiled his sons in a way he, and the nanny he had not hired yet, would have a hard time to undo.

* * *

Paul left the motorway and stopped at a petrol station to fill up and roll back the car's soft top. He looked at the map and decided where to spend the first night. He loved water; he had heard of an alpine lake called "Lago di Brains" by the Italians and "Pragser Wildsee" by the Austrians. He drove for a couple of hours, concentrating on the road and taking in the scenery, stopping from time to time to soak in the view. He loved the river, the wood, the mountains or just the intense blue of the sky. He finally reached the lake and found a hotel with a view. They had a room available, so he decided to spend two nights there on impulse. Somehow he had reached his destination. He had coffee and a cake on the terrace overlooking the lake; it was almost the landscape of his dream, except the lake in his dream was larger. He started a mental conversation with his wife; she would have loved the view but probably thought the place was too remote. Even if they had been living in Italy, the logistics would make this trip complicated to repeat, yet he promised himself he would take his sons there and tell them about his dream from the terrace of this hotel. His room was ready; he took a shower, changed and decided to go for a walk.

* * *

The village was very small; he found a path near the lake. He came across a gate by the lake with a "for sale" sign; he could tell there was a house behind some old trees, although he couldn't see it very well.

There was a small wooden pier with a boathouse on stilts. On an impulse, he decided to write down the number, return to his room and call the real estate agency.

We have to tell grandma

When my children were young, Friday night dinner was a family affair. It still is, but now they have their own lives, so it is unusual for me to have all of them on the same night. That particular Friday night, we had been discussing the trip to Venice for my mother's 90th birthday, and we quickly dealt with the logistics during the first part of the meal. My sons would take time off work during their sisters' half-term in February. That night, the whole menu was prepared so we could taste the pistachio cake Susan, my youngest child, had made. She was cutting the cake when Roy shared something with the family that turned Friday night dinner into a family meeting, one of those I had with my children since their mother died a few years earlier.

"Tom has never been to Venice; that would be a perfect time to show him where I was born."

Tom is Roy's long-term partner; they have been a couple for three years, and the whole family likes him, including Susan, who used to be extremely jealous of her big brother's partners. Roy is the only one of my children born in Venice.

Susan stopped cutting the cake.

"Where will Tom stay? He should stay with us, but we must tell grandma you are gay."

Tom had no idea that his partner's grandmother did not know that he was gay. For some reason, they all look at me.

"When Roy came out to us twenty years ago, your mother and I thought it was not our story to tell. So, do not look at me."

Roy looked at his partner, blushing.

"It never came up; in the past three years, I have never been in Venice for more than a couple of days and never with you. I was either enjoying being spoiled by my grandmother or concerned about her health; it never happened."

Roy's other sister, Yael, was equally shocked. Usually, her big brother could do nothing wrong, but this time she was not so sure.

"It never came up in the three years you have been with Tom?"

Roy was on the defensive.

"I know Grandma loves me, but I am also aware she turns 90 next February. A woman of her generation may not react the way I would hope."

Jonathan, my other son, thought he had a brilliant idea.

"Dad could tell her."

Susan was adamant that it should happen before we all left for Venice.

"I think it is a brilliant idea, Dad. You tell her."

At the end of the evening, I felt I had to apologise to Tom, who told me he felt part of the family; he was flattered that everybody wanted to introduce him to Roy's grandmother as Roy's partner.

So, the following Sunday morning, I called my mother. I explained our plans for her birthday and reassured her that Yael and Susan would not lose a day of school; then, I told her that Roy would come with his partner Tom. My mother's reaction was interesting; she gave me a lecture about why it should not matter to me. As per usual, when she was on a high horse, she would not allow anybody else to comment. At the end of a ten minutes tirade, she concluded by saying.

"Let's look at it from your point of you; it is none of your business whom Roy loves. Do you like his partner?"

I was happy to finally express my opinion after monosyllabic contributions to the conversation for the past ten minutes.

"We all like Tom. I could not care less whom Roy loves, as long as he is happy. Tom makes him happy and more at peace with himself than he has ever been. That is more than I could ask from Roy's partner, and I genuinely like Tom. You'll find him interesting, and you might even approve."

My mother faked indignation.

"Don't I always approve of my grandchildren's partners?"

"May I remind you of the words you and Susan used to describe Jonathan's former girlfriend?"

I could almost see my mother smiling and showing displeasure simultaneously.

"Well, she was a superficial and arrogant ignoramus who thought she had an encyclopaedic knowledge of everything and anything. Anyway, I am glad you like Tom, and I am looking forward to meeting him."

* * *

In a close extended family, people of different views frequently come together simply because they share DNA and memories. My large extended family consists of people with a wide variety of viewpoints; ironically, I get on very well with people with a vision of the world so different from mine that sometimes I wonder if we are related. These same people are among the first to rally around if there is a problem or the first to congratulate you for anything you celebrate.

My cousin Vera, is very conservative in her views. We live in two different galaxies, often having animated debates, but we respect each other.

A couple of weeks after I told my mother that Roy is gay, I called Vera to discuss my mother. Vera is very fond of her, and she is one of the several people who visit my mother at least once a week, sometimes more often. Vera had gone with my mother to an appointment with her cardiologist. We discussed my mother's general health and planning her 90th birthday party. Vera had to get off the water bus and would call me back as soon as possible. When she called back, she told me she had just had coffee with a friend. She hoped she did not offend her when she declined her invitation to her son's wedding.

"It is not really a wedding; it is a ceremony formalising the union between her youngest son and his boyfriend."

Vera and I disagree on the subject; we have already discussed it several times.

"I thought that civil unions were now legal in Italy."

Vera was slowly but steadily climbing on her high horse.

"They are, but I had to come up with an excuse to decline the invitation. Marriage can only be between a man and a woman, I have nothing against a gay couple, but there is a difference between the sanctity of a ceremony uniting a man and a woman in marriage and a civil servant putting a metaphorical stamp on the union between two men or two women."

I should make non-committal noises but I have never avoided a debate with Vera. She is two years younger than I am, and we have debated our opposite views on many things for more than sixty years.

"What is your view about the 'sanctity' of a civil servant putting a metaphorical stamp on the union of a man and a woman?"

Vera was undeterred.

"My problem is not with a marriage at City Hall instead of a synagogue or a church. My problem is calling a union between two men or two women a marriage, and I cannot attend a ceremony that endorses that."

The conversation ended because Vera was about to enter a shop. I wondered what could happen when Roy decided to get married. He will definitely marry a man.

* * *

The trip to Venice for my mother's 90th birthday was a success. Tom was also a success; to my surprise, even my family's most conservative members embraced him wholeheartedly. The general consensus was that he was a lovely person and a perfect fit for Roy. Vera even told Roy he would be foolish to let Tom go.

One Sunday, a couple of weeks after we were back from Venice, the phone rang at 5.30 am; I could see it was my mother's number. I did not feel very social at that time in the morning; I am sure it was reflected in my tone of voice.

"What happened?"

My mother sounded full of energy.

"Nothing happened; I woke up at 4 am and could not go back to sleep, so I started reading yesterday's paper. I had no idea that civil partnerships were now legal in Italy; Roy and Tom could get married here."

I was most definitely not wide awake.

"Mum, it Is 5.30 am on a Sunday; why are you telling me these things?"

My mother's energy almost hurt.

"Because you can tell Roy that he can transfer his residence here without a problem; after all, he is also an Italian citizen; Tom can come as his fiancé, and we could have the reception on my terrace if it is warm enough."

I still had not come to terms with waking up early on a Sunday morning.

"So, why did you ring me? You have Roy's number and could have woken him up."

"Because you are his father, and I am his grandmother. It is a father and son conversation; it is most definitely not for a grandmother to discuss her grandson's plans to get married or why there are no such plans."

At that stage, I was ready to say anything to go back to sleep.

"I will, and I'll call you later; bye."

Later in the day, when I called her, neither of us mentioned our early morning conversation.

* * *

I am in Venice to visit my mother almost three months after that conversation. I have to organise her journey to London for Roy and

Tom's wedding. I am sitting at a table at my favourite place in Venice, Nico at Zattere, the best ice cream place in Venice. I am waiting for Vera. I need to discuss who will take my mother to London when Roy and Tom get married. I also have to invite her and her family, because it wouldn't be a family celebration without her.

She arrived fashionably late and immaculately turned out like any member of my mother's family. We start discussing what she thinks my mother will need in the near future. When we have finished discussing my mother's requirements, it is time for me to bring up an October wedding in London.

"There is another thing I need to ask. Would you be available to come to London with my mother in October?"

"What is the occasion?"

Here we go. I try to sip from an empty espresso cup just to buy time.

"Roy and Tom are getting married."

Vera does not even blink; her reaction is immediate.

"Roy is smart; I told him he should not be foolish and let Tom go. Good on him for deciding to marry him. Did you meet Tom's parents?'

Who is this woman sitting in front of me, and what has she done with my cousin Vera? I have to share something Tom is not very keen to share.

"Unfortunately not. Tom does not have any contact with his family anymore."

Vera does not react the way I expected.

"This is a disgrace; whatever they think of homosexuality, Tom is their son."

There is a pause; she is thinking of something. Her body language and facial expression resemble my mother's when she is formulating a plan. I almost don't hear what she asks me or what she tells me to do.

` " Give me your phone. I need to talk to Roy."

Vera's tone of voice is very similar to my mother's. You question an Italian Jewish mother on a mission at your own risk, so I give her my phone, and she calls Roy. After a very brief exchange, she comes to the point.

"Is Tom around? Can you put the phone on speaker and translate for him?"

Roy must have confirmed that Tom was with him; after a pause, Vera continued.

"Roy, please apologise to Tom on my behalf, I am going to get personal, and I accept if he tells me that is none of my business. I would also like both of you to understand that I have been fond of you all your life and like Tom."

As Roy translates, I sit there steeling myself for a tirade about the sanctity of marriage between a man and a woman; Vera surprises me.

"Roy, can you please tell Tom that if he still does not talk to his parents by the time you get married, I'll be honoured if he allows me and my husband to act as his parents and all my family to sit on his side of the aisle when you get married."

There is a pause; Vera tells me that she can hear Tom reacting to Roy's translation, but her English is not good enough. Then Roy comes back on the phone.

"Vera, Tom is very touched. He is too emotional to speak but has been nodding, so I take it as a yes. I am touched as well. Hugs to all the family."

"Great, I'll bring your grandma to London with us. I'll let you go now; big hugs to you and Tom."

I sit there stunned; my cousin surprised me. My face must be a huge question mark. I have to ask.

"Weren't you lecturing anybody willing to listen about the sanctity of marriage between a man and a woman? Last time I checked, Roy and Tom are both men."

Vera gives me back the phone; she adjusts her scarf and moves her handbag, buying time to organise her thoughts.

"I still think so, but there are three considerations (1) nothing would make me disown my children; I cannot understand how you can stop loving your child. Tom likes men, so what? It is none of his parents' business. They should be happy for him as long as he is with someone who makes him happy. (2) I am very fond of Roy, and (3) I like Tom, and I think he is good for Roy; when they were here, I told Roy that he should stop sitting on the fence and marry him. I am happy he listened to my advice."

She then smiles and turns to me.

"By now, you should know that our family does not put terms and conditions on love. We take our own as they are; Tom will become one of our own, therefore..."

She stops and just grins like the Cheshire Cat in Alice in Wonderland. Her final words make me smile.

"Oh, tell Tom we shall come to London between now and October; we need to know him better if we must act as his family."

I am not sure Tom knows what is about to hit him; I hope he will still be touched after he has faced Vera on a mission.

Acknowledgments

I wrote these stories while working on other writing projects that still need to be completed. I wrote a short story when I was fed up with editing and revising. Other times I stopped everything because "a story took root in my brain".

Several people are responsible for my transformation into a writer. Andrea Rosen, my eldest son Eyal, and my close friend Maria Vittoria believed in my voice when it was still very tentative. Lynne Halliday gave me a well-deserved kick on the backside and made me think of the quality of my sentences; if you do not get bored reading what I write, you owe it to her. A special place is reserved for the wonderful creators of the London Writer Salons, Matt Trinetti and Parul-Barvishi. What started as an experiment at the beginning of the first lockdown became a global community that has increased the quality of my life, brought me new friends, and helped me become a better and more confident writer, and what's more it is still going strong three years later.

The LWS community has critiqued these stories in various ways. Thank you, Abbey Vint and Kathryn Koromilas (KK), for running the critique sessions; Monica Camara, Rachel Powell, Gina Beach, Patricia Lane, Emily Reid, and KK for running the open mike sessions. Sue DuFeu, Barrie Tankel, Sofia Koutlaki, Marian Green, Konrad, and many, many others, too many to mention, for all the comments and feedback in the chat of those zoom sessions. You made me a confident writer.

Last but not least, I need to thank those who encouraged and took me seriously in the past three years, so thank you, Alessandra Bellini, Alessandro Saporetti, Anna Rita Cartolari, Silvio Gatta, Michelle Nordell, David Nordell, Daniella Pinkstein, Jonathan Beloff, Shalom Morris, Steve Rosenzweig, Sharon Rosenzweig Kaplan and my whole family.

Coming Soon: The Dressmaker's Parcels

Here follows the introduction and the first two chapters of "The Dressmaker's Parcel", a story based on how Fascist Italy's racial laws impacted my mother's family and inspired by my mother and grandmother's involvement with the Italian resistance during the last 18 months of World War II. The book will be available on several platforms from mid-May 2023, it will also be possible to order it from bookstores.

Introduction

Venice February 2014

Emma Mendes Sonnino's four grandchildren were in Venice at the same time, she loved it and thought it was the best part of turning 90. It was not the exact date of her birthday; she had decided that her granddaughters should not miss school. School was too precious for her; at 90, she could still get emotional about being forced to leave her school by Mussolini's racial laws 76 years earlier when she was 14. She decided to celebrate her birthday when school in the United Kingdom had half-term holidays.

Emma could make her presence felt by just being in the room, and she was never loud or flamboyant. Somebody who could show her approval – or disapproval – with a look but whose smile could light up the night and make you feel loved and supported; she was a woman of substance, not a woman of noise. Many people had helped organise a celebratory weekend with forty guests, but nobody made a big fuss about it. They knew it was not her style.

That Thursday afternoon, Emma was enjoying being in the same room as her four grandchildren; they were all doing their own thing. Roy, her eldest grandson and his partner were working, Jonathan, 25, was reading, and Yael and Lisa were looking at vintage fashion magazines.

Her son walked into the room with the mail. He gave the letters to his mother, thinking they were just birthday cards from her many cousins scattered around the world. Her youngest grandchild, Lisa, looked at the letter Emma had opened and put it on the coffee table next to the armchair where she was sitting.

"Grandma, why are you invited to a ceremony for the seventieth anniversary of the liberation of Rome?"

Emma picked up the letter again, read it, and then turned to her granddaughter.

"Well, they say here that they want to celebrate the Italian Jews who fought in the resistance and are still alive."

Roy, her eldest grandson, lifted his head from his laptop.

"Am I the only one who knows you were in the resistance? I can't believe you never told them."

Emma smiled; she gestured for her grandchildren to come closer and sit near her. Roy, his partner, and Jonathan sat on the floor, Yael and Lisa in the other two armchairs.

"I was not the only one in my family. It all started when my mother, your great-grandmother, found out she was pregnant with your aunt Mila eight years after the birth of her fifth child...."

Chapter One

Venice September 1942

It was love at first sight when Gabriele and Rachele met one Friday night in 1920. Twenty-one years of marriage and five children later, they could still feel better just being next to each other. Walking together around Venice improved their mood; they could face everything together. The war, racial laws, the need to re-invent themselves professionally when they lost their jobs because they were Jewish, and being concerned about their children's future had not changed how they related to each other.

They had been walking in total silence for the past twenty minutes. Silence between them was never uncomfortable; they were trying to absorb what they had heard half an hour earlier. It was not early menopause; Rachele was expecting their sixth child. They had arranged to see their closest non-Jewish friends, Paolo and Sofia Mondani, for pre-dinner drinks. It was a mild September late afternoon, and the oppressive heat and humidity of the summer were long

1

forgotten. When they reached the Rialto fish market, Rachele stopped, turned to her husband, and broke the silence.

"A child at our age with everything that is going on, what do you think?"

Gabriele took some time to organise his thoughts. He had not yet come to terms with the need to use different names for the hospital appointment. The racial laws prevented Rachele from seeing a non-Jewish doctor; it was not an emergency. The appointment was made under Sofia Taiman Mondani instead of Rachele Modiano Mendes. At that moment, he was just enjoying being next to his wife. The only thing on his mind was that twenty- two years earlier, he got lost in the green of her eyes, and he could still get lost in the green of her eyes.

"I am excited and angry at the same time; excited because of the new life we have created, angry because we had to see a friend of Paolo's at the hospital who knew very well who we were but kept calling us Paolo and Sofia. However, when I stop thinking of those things, I am excited and worried about you."

At that moment, Rachele was more worried over the lingering smell of fish that was playing dirty tricks on her stomach. She put her arm around Gabriele's and pulled him towards their friends' home.

They had waited until after dinner to tell the rest of the family, and the general excitement had delayed everybody's bedtime.

Rachele could not sleep. She did not want to wake up her husband. She quietly got up and walked to the kitchen, making as little noise as possible, hoping a hot drink would help her fall asleep. They kept mint on the kitchen windowsill; mint tea was infinitely better than any coffee or tea surrogate they had tried in the past. Somehow she was not surprised when Anita joined her. Anita was their live-in housekeeper and her most loyal friend and confidante. The third most important adult in their household, the woman their children loved and called 'aunt.' They had shared a hot drink in the kitchen and their concerns several times in the middle of the night. Anita asked Rachele why she could not sleep. Usually, Rachele was not very talkative, but that night was different.

"I am fed up. Today was the final straw. I had to pretend I was Sofia. The doctor knew I was not, but he also had to pretend. I want to use this time to think about what I can do to change things, whatever contribution I can make to end this mess, so I can start when the baby is eight months."

Anita had not heard such fighting talk before; she did not know what to say. Rachele continued

"I have had enough. We have been trying to adjust for four years. First, our children could not go to school with non-Jewish children, then we lost our jobs and had to invent another way of making a living, then we had to protect our home. By the way, I am eternally grateful for your help. I won't do anything now, but I will take this time to figure out what I can do."

Anita nodded. They both drank their mint tea, sighed, and spent some time in silence, then Rachele stood up.

"Good night Anita; thank you for listening. You and Gabriele are my rocks. I think I'll try to catch some sleep now."

Venice November 1942

Alvise Cantoni and Gabriele Mendes had been friends for a long time. When Alvise met Rachele, one of the few women to practice law in the Kingdom of Italy, they bonded immediately over their shared professional interests. They began working together when they lost their jobs due to racial laws. Rachele's law firm had found a way to make use of them. They were preparing cases and checking legal documents. It was a mutually beneficial arrangement. Alvise and Rachele could still earn money; the law firm used two experienced lawyers as glorified legal secretaries. They were getting their experience at a considerably lower cost. When war broke out, their workload increased. With most young men in the armed forces, Alvise and Rachele did all the work except discussing cases in court or publicly meeting clients. They were working independently but occasionally met to discuss cases. That morning Alvise noticed that Rachele was very annoyed.

"When I was expecting Davide, this was the time I stopped accepting new cases. I did not want to leave anything unresolved before I had the baby. Now there is nothing to leave unresolved. We are doing the boring part of our job. I miss dealing with clients; I miss being in court. I am fed up. Once this baby is eight months old, I need to start doing something to change all this."

"Well, talk to me when you are ready. I might know somebody who is in a position to help."

Rachele smiled at Alvise's caution.

"Great, because at the moment, I even miss being mistaken for my secretary."

Venice, February 1943

Venice Jewish schools did not go any further than middle school, and Emma and Anna did not want to stay with their uncle in Milan or their mother's cousin in Geneva to continue their education. They

4

had taken a few days off work to help sort out the nursery. Emma worked for one of her father's clients, Mrs Toffolo; she had just been promoted from apprentice to junior seamstress. Anna was learning to be a master baker. They had been cleaning the small room next to their parents' bedroom for a while when Anita appeared with mint tea and some biscuits made by Rachele the previous day. She was all dressed up; the two young women started teasing their honorary aunt. They noticed Anita's face and stopped. Anna was the first to ask what was wrong. Anita did not usually share "grown-up problems" with the children, but Emma and Anna were nineteen and seventeen, old enough to understand.

"Usually, I try to forget the war, those stupid laws, and everything else and just think of what needs to be done on the day. Today what I have to do reminds me of what I usually try very hard to forget."

Emma stopped emptying a chest of drawers, turned back, took one of the small plates from the tray, and started putting biscuits on it.

"Where are you going?"

" I meet the court officer who has to agree to my guardianship of the unborn baby, who will be delivered by a woman that does not wish to be named but whose identity is guaranteed by Giorgio Falier. To maintain client confidentiality, he will be at the hospital during birth to confirm that the baby in question is the one for whom I have guardianship."

Anita also told them that she was trying not to discuss it with their mother; she was sure Rachele knew all about it, but she was due two weeks later, and she needed to be as calm and relaxed as possible, given the circumstances.

Venice, March 1943

Rachele had already given birth to five children. She knew what to expect and was not keen to go to the hospital. However, this time, the doctor kept mentioning her age and possible complications for her and the baby. The Jewish midwife who saw her every week thought that the baby might be in an awkward position. She agreed with the doctor. In the end, Rachele was convinced, but the ruse they had to put in place for her to go to the hospital made her even more determined to be a proactive agent of change as soon as possible.

She hated the 'confidential' arrangement generally used by women who wanted to hide that they had a baby. In her case, hiding her identity was a way to protect her and the doctor. A non-Jewish doctor could not treat her, and her hospital admission was not due to an emergency. They were in clear breach of the racial laws. She hated that Gabriele could not visit her or be in the waiting room. Giorgio Falier was there to confirm that the baby born from Rachele was the one mentioned in Anita's guardianship papers; Anita was there as well.

In the end, everything went smoothly, and a baby girl was born. They called her Mila, and the court gave her a last name until somebody filed adoption papers. Gabriele had to stay away to keep up with the "mother who does not wish to be named" story. Officially, Anita had come to take the baby away; nobody pointed out that she had left the hospital with Rachele. Too many people were aware that she was a friend of Doctor Paolo Mondani.

Gabriele's youngest brother, Roberto, was helping Emma make sure that the nursery was ready for the new baby; Emma was nineteen years older than her new sibling. She always considered Roberto as an older brother more than an uncle. In her eyes, he had always been considerably younger than the "other grown-ups." She could not hide her frustration from him.

"I am fed up with adjusting; I am fed up with just surviving, hoping that the war will end and those stupid laws will not exist anymore. I wish I could do something; we should all be doing something."

Roberto was smiling inwardly; he was not ready to tell his niece that he was indeed "doing something."

Emma could not stop venting her frustration.

"I remember how different things were when Davide was born. The Modiano grandparents came from Trieste. They did not need permission from any authority; they just bought the ticket and came. It was not secretive at all. Now my youngest sister does not even have my last name. Also, I should be studying hard for my *"esame di maturita',,* [1] looking forward to studying law at the University and becoming a lawyer like my mother. Because of all those stupid laws, I must be grateful to work at Mrs Toffolo to make clothes for ladies who are not supposed to know I am Jewish. Uncle Roberto, I have really had enough."

Emma's uncle was surprised by her outburst. He lifted his head from the cot he was cleaning,

"I thought you liked working with materials; I remember fondly your spending hours in the family warehouse gently caressing those rolls of printed silk."

Emma stopped putting the baby's clothes away; she put down the tiny shirts she was holding, put her hands on her hips and assumed a very determined and confident pose.

"I love it, but I also love reading and studying. Mum loves baking, but she practices law; I thought I would practice law and work with materials as a hobby. I may not end up studying law, but I want to

7

do something to change where the country is going. Will you help me?"

"Well, I know somebody who could help. Let's leave it for a while; think about it for three months. If you still want to do something by the end of June, I'll talk to my friends."

"His friends" were none other than himself, Emma's honorary uncle Paolo Mondani, his daughter-in-law Carolina Rinaldi Mondani, and Alvise Cantoni, her mother's unofficial business partner and her father's close friend. Roberto was just not prepared to share that with his niece yet.

Chapter Two

1936-1938

July 1936

There were only a handful of women practicing law in the kingdom of Italy, and none of them had five children! Gabriele loved starting the day walking to work with his wife. Their relatively small height difference was made even smaller by her heels, her green eyes looking at him each time she stopped walking to make a point. They left earlier than usual to enjoy the relatively cool air before the summer heat and humidity made walking unpleasant. It was their private time.

Rachele's office was past the Rialto bridge, near the Fondaco dei Tedeschi. She had been working there since she got married and moved to Venice fifteen years earlier. Her good mood ended after her phone rang for the umpteenth time that morning.

. . .

"Could you put me through to Avvocato[1[Modiano, please? I asked to speak to him and not to his secretary."

"I am Avvocato Modiano," replied Rachele with a stern tone of voice. The caller 'regrouped' after a short silence; the conversation was very productive, and, in the end, he apologised.

She met her husband by the Rialto bridge to walk home for lunch. Fifteen years and five children later, his smile could still improve the worst of her mood. Gabriele noticed she was annoyed.

"Challenging day at work?" he said after kissing her on the cheek

"Somebody mistook me for my secretary yet again."

Rachele let off steam during their walk home. She was aware that she and her sisters were an oddity, women who kept working even after they got married and had children, they were even more of an oddity because they did not need to work. She was grateful that it did not matter to Gabriele that she earned more money than he did. As they approached Campo San Giacomo dall'Orio her mood improved. She felt privileged that she and Gabriele were a true partnership, two individuals who choose to be together every day.

They climbed the two flight of steps to their front door. When they opened it, the aromas of lunch hit them. Leo, Diana, and Anna raced to hug them. Anita came out of the kitchen to greet them, saying that lunch would be ready when Emma arrived back from school. Gabriele smiled, Rachele smiled back. It was the life they wanted; everything else did not matter.

October 1937

Emma and her parents had gone to the station to meet the train from Vienna. Her aunt Barbara, her husband, and their three children would spend two nights in Venice before boarding a ship to Australia. Emma was there to allow the grown-ups to talk away from younger people's ears. She convinced the other children to follow the porter whose cart had all the luggage.

Rachele asked her sister what their plans were; it was her tactful way to figure out why they had picked Australia. Barbara was expecting the question; she had the same conversation several times in the previous months. They were going to sail to Alexandria, wait a day there and board another ship to Singapore. After a few days, they would board another ship to Brisbane, their final destination. Barbara started working at the hospital as head of their laboratory two months after they arrived. Rachele saw a possible way to find out what she wanted to find out.

"How did you get the job?"

Barbara was delighted to change the subject

"I am not sure whether I was more surprised when they offered me a job, or they were when they read that the most senior researcher at the Imperial College in London had recommended a woman."

Rachele had used the diversionary tactic she often used in court. She then moved to what she really wanted to find out

"So, you are moving to Australia for your job...."

By now, Barbara had figured out what her sister wanted to know.

"Herbert did not get his promotion because he was Jewish. When I received the letter, I replied that I would come with a husband and three children if they were still interested. Six weeks later, they answered me that they were. The following day David was almost beaten up on his way home from school. We started the paperwork two days after receiving the letter offering me a job. Herbert resigned. We sold our home. I am excited; it is a new adventure."

Rachele was quiet for a bit, taking in what her sister had said.

"How did Herbert's parents react?"

"They think we should have made alyah[2] or go to the United States. They consider Australia a rough place, full of convicts and at the edge of civilisation."

"And is it?"

"I hope not; we have already contacted the Jewish community in Brisbane. They have painted a fairly civilised picture. It is as far away from Europe as we can possibly go. I want these few days to be happy and serene. God only knows when we'll see you and our parents again!"

They were approaching the final bridge leading to Campo San Giacomo Dall'Orio. Rachele noticed that Emma was busy showing the children how the porter was manoeuvring the cart with the luggage up and down the steps crossing a bridge.

As they were approaching their home, Gabriele noticed that Anita had sent down the young (and pretty) maid to wait for them; she probably reckoned that the porter would not allow a good-looking girl to carry the luggage to the first floor flat and would do it himself.

When they entered the flat, the conversation stopped. The guests had to be shown their accommodations; Anita had prepared something nice to eat with tea or coffee and appropriate drinks for the children. Once you walked into Gabriele and Rachele's home, you left the outside world outside.

* * *

The following morning Davide and Esther Modiano, Rachele's parents, arrived from Trieste. Anita had been Gabriele and Rachele's housekeeper for more than ten years, but she was still amazed by how Esther Coronel Modiano could enter a space and dominate it. Her posture and the way she walked matched Anita's ideas of a sovereign inspecting her land. And yet, Esther would not hesitate to wear a pair of rubber gloves and do the dishes or sweep the floor if that was what was needed. Anita loved her pragmatism, her common touch, and her class. She usually referred to her as "a woman of presence, not a woman of noise"; somebody who treats everybody in the same way, from the Emperor to the porter walking with them from the station. Her Italian was fluent, but her German accent was still very strong after fifty years.

"Anita, good morning; how nice to see you. We woke up very early to catch the first train to Venice, and I can barely keep my eyes open. Can I make coffee?"

Anita still admired how Baroness Esther Modiano could waltz in and immediately pick up what had to be done – or, in this case, what she needed most to be done – leaving her husband to pay the porter, sort the luggage and walk to the guest bedroom with the maid. Barbara appeared in the hall and welcomed her mother, which gave Anita some time to organise coffee and biscuits. Esther stopped to greet her daughter and did not walk into the kitchen to look for an apron and make coffee, probably still wearing her coat and hat.

Barbara and Herbert were now at the mercy of Esther's inquisitive mind. They were sitting in the large sitting room, the one with a view on Campo San Giacomo Dall'Orio, sipping yet another cup of coffee with some of the biscuits that Rachele, Anna, and Anita had baked the previous day. Esther knew no subtlety when she wanted to know something.

"So, what is the real reason why you are moving to the other side of the world?"

* * *

Later in the day, people started arriving for dinner. Herbert and Barbara were overwhelmed by how many had come to Venice to wish them well. Barbara's siblings had arrived from Trieste and Milan, some of their cousins from Rome, Trieste, Geneva, and Spalato.

* * *

It was time to leave Europe. They were not due on board until five. Herbert, Gabriele, and their father-in-law had gone to the station to collect the two steamers' trunks sent from Vienna. Before crossing the Grand Canal, Herbert stopped and turned to his father-in-law.

"Baron Modiano, Gabriele, I never expected such a crowd. It was very moving that everybody came to Venice just to say goodbye to us."

Baron Modiano stopped for a moment and put his arms on Herbert's shoulders.

"Herbert, we are used to people in other parts of the Mediterranean, but you are going to the other side of the world, almost literally. By the way, Haifa is your second port of call ... Gabriele, what are the names Greta and her husband are using now? "

"They are Ruth and Chaim, Baron Modiano"

"All right, Ruth and Chaim – what was wrong with Greta and Michele? –will be at Haifa harbour to take all five of you to lunch."

The three men walked in silence until Herbert stopped and turned to his father-in-law.

"Baron Modiano, I am sorry I am taking your daughter and your grandchildren so far away."

"Herbert, anything involving a Modiano woman can only be a joint decision. The two of you are taking my grandchildren to the other side of the world! But tell me, why Australia? Wasn't the Holy Land far enough?"

"We are just following an amazing job opportunity. It was coincidental that the job offer arrived the day before we decided to leave Vienna, and indeed Europe."

Baron Modiano turned to Gabriele and whispered, "We better act as if we believe them!

Early April 1938

Rachele was concentrating on a contract with her door open when she felt observed. She raised her head to see the senior partner in the firm standing at the door. As he walked inside the room, he noticed a magazine on top of her handbag.

"I had no idea you were reading that magazine."

"I don't; I just saw a headline that grabbed my interest and wanted to see what they were writing."

Rachele had asked him if he had time to discuss a contract with her, there was something that was not right, but she could not pin it down. Her boss could not help notice the title on the cover. He asked her what she thought. Rachele told him it reminded her of her brother-in-law Herbert who had been bypassed for promotion in Vienna the previous year because he was Jewish. Herbert, her sister Barbara and their children now lived in Australia. Her boss reacted using a reassuring tone of voice, or so he hoped.

"You know I would not do anything like that. I hired you, watched you grow professionally and personally; you are safe here."

"It is not that. Barbara and Herbert emigrated because they stopped feeling safe in Vienna. After they left, I had a conversation with my older daughter about how safe we felt in Venice. Will we still feel safe in Venice next month? Yesterday Gabriele overheard a stupid comment about their Jewish legal counsel. Somebody mentioned that Alvise Cantoni was not a real Venetian."

"The son of the "Doge of the Ghetto" not a real Venetian? They do not know what they are talking about."

Rachele smiled at the last comment; she stood up to pick up the magazine.

"Still, it is not relevant. I have not read the article yet, but I am beginning to wonder what would make me, or a member of my family, stop feeling safe in Venice."

"Venice is a bubble, the *Ponte Littorio*[3] is yet another evidence that Venice only has a tenuous link to the mainland. Therefore we are free from whatever stupid and dogmatic idea is fashionable there; you will always be safe here."

Rachele sat down again, it was nice to hear those reassuring words from the person who had faith in her all those years ago, but that was not entirely her point.

"Thank you, but I have started wondering, and I do not like it. I do not like the idea that my children might grow up with a sense of insecurity, that they might feel that they do not fit in in the place where they were born. But you are here to discuss this contract; let's see if two heads are better than one."

Their discussion of the contract revealed Rachele's doubts; her boss said she could probably use a break from it. She ordered a coffee and read the magazine for ten minutes. The article intellectually annoyed and emotionally concerned her. Rachele rang her husband to say she would leave the office early; she just needed fresh air.

She loved the springtime weather in Venice. She walked to clear her head, her surrounding slightly out of focus like an impressionist painting. She wandered aimlessly, but she was not lost. It was just a longer route home. She turned left after Rialto Bridge, walked along the Grand Canal for a while, then turned right through countless narrow streets, bridges crossing narrow and wider canals. She found herself in Campo San Polo, and about an hour after leaving the office, she arrived outside the front door of her home in Campo San Giacomo Dall'Orio. She still had not decided how to react to the article that annoyed her so much, but she had figured out what to do about the contract she had been reading for most of her day. She would discuss the article with Gabriele in the privacy of their bedroom, or they would take one of those after-dinner walks they both loved so much.

15 April 1938 - First night of Passover

It was a long-standing tradition that the Mendes clan would gather together the first night of Passover. Gabriele's eldest brother, Raffaele, and his wife, Antonella, were the hosts this year. At the end of the Seder[4], they told the family they had decided to leave Italy.

Gabriele and Rachele were enjoying the walk home. Anna was walking silently between her parents, until

"Will we leave Venice as well? Last year it was Uncle Herbert and Aunt Barbara, this year it is Uncle Raffaele, Aunt Antonella with Carlo, Fiamma and Andrea. Are we going as well?"

Rachele and Gabriele looked at each other; she nodded, so he answered.

"Would you like to leave?"

"I love my world as is, and I love living in Venice. This evening Grandpa said that our ancestors had been involved in printing and dying silk for almost four hundred years. Venice is our home; why should we leave?"

Gabriele hoped he was going to sound reassuring.

"People move because their job takes them elsewhere, they want to explore new possibilities, or they want to be with the person they love."

"Like mummy moved from Trieste to Venice."

"Exactly – continued Rachele – and when you are grown up, you may decide to move for any of those reasons."

"During the centuries our family has lived in Venice – continued Gabriele – there have been hard times and easy times, but we were never forced to leave or to stop being Jewish. It is a privilege compared to other parts of Europe. We may visit your Modiano grandparents in Trieste, or spend some time in the mountains, or go to the beach, or go somewhere else, but we shall always come home, back to our Campo in Venice."

About the Author

Silvano Stagni is a multilingual citizen of the world, a father of four, and a cosmopolitan character with a long and varied life. In his youth, he was blessed to have many storytellers, people from different cultures and walks of life. He heard stories from the Imperial Court in Vienna, stories from the Kenyan bush, stories of seafarers, stories of survivors, and stories of fighters. He started writing articles, white papers and opinion pieces during his previous professional life as an expert in the implementation of financial regulations. Now it is his turn to tell stories.

Check Silvano's Newsletter:
https://authorsilvano.substack.com/

Notes

The quintet

1. *Babu* means paternal grandfather in Swahili

Chapter 1

1. This is the name of the exam at the end of the Italian high school; a pass would allow the student to attend University. According to Mussolini's racial laws, Jewish students could only finish high school in Milan or Rome and attend University abroad.

Chapter 2

1. "Avvocato" in Italian means 'lawyer'. If you have passed the Italian equivalent of the bar and you are a practicing lawyer, it is common to use your job as a title. Nowadays, it would be considered a very formal way of answering the phone, and many people would just use their name.
2. Make aliyah, i.e. emigrate to the Holy Land. What is now Israel and what was then part of the British Mandate in the Middle East.
3. Ponte Littorio was the name given to the road bridge that connects Venice to the mainland when it was opened in 1933. After World War II, it was renamed "Ponte della Liberta'" (Bridge of Freedom). The Austrian built the railway bridge next to it in 1846; it was expanded to its current width in the 1970s.
4. The Seder is the Passover ceremonial dinner held in memory of the Jewish slaves leaving Egypt and crossing the Red Sea

www.ingramcontent.com/pod-product-compliance
Lightning Source LLC
Chambersburg PA
CBHW030642130626
46552CB00002B/971